The Boys of Calderfield College
For the Love of Jock Pussy

The Boys of Calderfield College
For the Love of Jock Pussy

Christopher Trevor

SEVENTH WINDOW

For the Love of Jock Pussy © 2013 Christopher Trevor

This is entirely a work of fiction. This is not a guide for safe sex practices. Any resemblance to actual persons, living or dead, events or locales is entirely coincidental.

First Seventh Window Publications edition: April 2013

Published in the United States of America by:
Seventh Window Publications
P.O. BOX 603165
Providence, RI 02906-0165

http://www.SeventhWindow.com

ISBN: 978-0-9896060-0-4

"Life must be lived forward, but can only be understood backwards."
Søren Kierkegaard
(1813 – 1855)

1

"Oooooo," Travis Bradley O'Toole the fourth groaned in a high-pitched crescendo as John, his blackmailing and so-called college buddy, greased his bunghole with old-fashioned Crisco shortening. Travis was sprawled out on the floor of John's dorm room wearing just his white knee high sweat socks by Nike and a red jockstrap from International Male, left over from the recent college football game. Travis was sprawled on his hands and knees, with his delectable, well-shaped and muscular butt high in the air, giving John easy access to it for the plans he had.

"Oh, you bastard, John, my poor, smelly asshole. What's the point of all this?" Travis squabbled miserably as the blackmailer used three and then four fingers at a time to really slop the Crisco into his prize's rectal hole.

John's vision of Travis' muscular butt cheeks on display with the strap from his red sweat scented jockstrap under them, and his big kiwi-sized balls dangling and encased in the pouch of the jockstrap, was beyond electric. Also, the smell emanating from Travis' asshole was intoxicating to John as he breathed it in. It was the scent of captivity, the scent of fear from the man he had so easily ensnared via a video. And if Travis only knew the main reason that John delighted in having him under his thumb, well, the blackmailer doubted that the handsome jock would even believe it. John himself could not believe how the fates had been so kind to deliver Travis Bradley O' Tool the fourth to him in such a fashion. It was what he had been waiting for since he had found out that the jock was attending the prestigious Calderfield College; and now the fourth was paying for what the third had done. Ah, but revenge was so sweet, and as the saying went, a dish best served cold. But in this case, revenge was a dish being served in Travis' hot, raw, and stinking asshole.

"Fun, O'Toole, lighthearted fun, that's the point of all this, and I have to admit it's always been a fantasy of mine to congratulate a hero football player in this manner," John said gleefully, then slid three greased fingers into Travis' hole, wriggling them around in there not all that gently and getting more grunts and gasping sounds from the prize sprawled on the floor. "And God knows you football jocks sure do have the most interesting ways of congratulating each other; and seeing as you were the hero of today's game, well, it's only right that you *should be* congratulated."

Travis clenched his teeth tight, curled his toes back in his white sweat socks and squinted as he felt John's greasy, Crisco slicked fingertips caressing and massaging his ass walls. The jock was ashamed to admit that his cock was beginning to bulge the front of his musty jockstrap. Travis hated what John was doing to him, taking liberties in ways that no one should be doing to him *or* to anyone, for that matter. But the handsomer than handsome jock could not deny that whenever his asshole was toyed with, or even fucked (My God, what had he come to, he wondered?) for that matter, he seemed to pop a hard-on.

Beads of piss mixed with pre-cum stained the sweat soaked jockstrap Travis was wearing as he felt John's damned fingertips stroking his ass walls.

"Fucker, us football players pat each other on the padded butt to congratulate each other on great plays, we pick up a guy who made a touchdown and give him a victory ride off the field on our big shoulders, just like my buds did to me earlier today. It's a heady feeling being carried off the field that way, man, makes a guy feel like a king of sorts. We also spray each other with expensive champagne in the locker room, we douse our coach with ice and Gatorade, we do all the things we did after today's game, I might add. But, I've never, *ever* heard of greasing and prodding a football player's stink hole with Crisco as a way to applaud him, uhhhhhhh, easy with my back door, huh John?" Travis quibbled miserably.

"I suppose you could say then that I've started a new tradition here, O'Toole. You'll have to tell all your football buddies about it, and how much you enjoyed it," John said with a laugh as he reached under Travis with his other hand and gave his hardening jockstrap covered cock a good squeeze. "This hard-on of yours is testament to how much you're enjoying what I'm doing to you here, bud. And I'm sure that once you tell your fellow football jocks on the team and even your suited buddies about the new tradition of greasing a dudes asshole after a good play, well, somehow I get the feeling that you'll be spending a lot of time in the position I have you in now.

Travis felt as if the blackmailing bastard was digging for gold in his most private crevice. And now, to make it worse, he was tormenting his nine inch pride and joy as well. The huge jar of Crisco brand shortening was on the floor next to Travis' muscular arms as he maintained his position on his hands and knees, the sight of the jar mocking him.

"I doubt that my football buds would see this as a way of being congratulated, John," Travis sniveled.

As he thought of his football buddies and the game that they had just played and won against a rival college team, Travis knew that they *would not* believe what John was doing to him. Actually, Travis knew that his buddies would not believe that he was actually *allowing* John to rummage around in his asshole like a gold digger of sorts. But with what John had on Travis, there was no way that the jock could refuse the blackmailer's demands. After making the touchdown that had won his team the game, it was Travis' good buddy, Bart Findley, also his suit man buddy, who had come charging over to Travis like a madman and hoisted him on his colossal shoulders and then did the honors of carrying the jock off the field. Amid the cheers from the crowd and the rest of the team whooping it up as Bart carted him off the field like a king, Travis felt a deep sense of elation.

But what Travis didn't know was that his skinhead Spike and his two black skinhead buddies, the muscular prison yard guys Jerome and Darren, were in the bleachers as well, and watching the game. Spike was taking a certain amount of pride in seeing his jock pussy boy being carried off the field by his buddy, Bart. And it was not lost on Spike either how Jerome and Darren were once again looking at Travis with raw animal lust. But Spike had already read them the riot act where *his* jock pussy boy was concerned. But that did not mean that Jerome and Darren weren't hungry for fresh jock boy meat, as they watched Bart Findley carry Spike's boy off the field on his shoulders.

In the locker room, after Bart sat Travis down, the celebrations continued with Travis being doused and sprayed with champagne and slapped hard on his padded butt cheeks as a few of his teammates took turns hoisting him to their giant shoulders and carrying him around the locker room a few times each.

Travis whooped and cheered and was feeling thrilled in the moment. He was thrilled until John made the scene in the locker room and quietly instructed Travis to be in his dorm room after all the festivities were over; and to make sure he was still wearing his jockstrap. Travis' feeling of being thrilled vanished instantly and was replaced with one of dismay as he watched John quickly exit the locker room. Travis had no doubt that he was in for more nastiness with John. Looking around, Travis was glad to see that none of his football buddies had heard what John had just said to him. They were either oblivious to the scuz-ball having entered their private domain, or they simply did not give a shit about what had been transpiring between John and Travis. All of them except Bart, who was slowly approaching Travis.

"Hey, buddy, what was that all about?" Bart asked, his deep voice gravelly and a bit raspy after all the cheering and manly screaming he had just done out on the football field. He approached Travis wearing a pair of tight fitting silk OTC navy blue sheer socks by Stacy Adams with garters clipped to them and sexy, tight fitting matching boxer briefs by International Male, having donned them after he had showered. "What did that wormy guy want? I've seen the way he looks at you, man. I mean, I don't mind the gay dudes checking out us suit men, it's a compliment after all, but I don't want any of them, especially that pile of shit, hitting on us, or for that matter, hitting on my best bud.

"Nothing, bud, nothing at all," Travis replied miserably as Bart ruffled his hair, a favorite thing to do where Travis was concerned. "Don't give it another thought."

"I won't, *he's not worth it,* c'mon, man, get into a power suit, some sheer socks and shoes and come to the mall. Us suit men are meeting there to celebrate the win."

"I—uh—I can't," Travis said. "I have a previous engagement."

"Yeah, and knowing you, its female, bud," Bart said with a laugh, then ruffled Travis' hair again and told him he would see him later, then walked back to his locker to finish getting dressed.

Travis watched as his exquisitely muscled buddy stepped around the corner and walked back to his locker, his tall silk socks and matching undershorts making Bart's muscularity all the more inviting. Travis grinned a bit, knowing how so many of the women on campus went totally bonkers over Bart.

But unseen by anyone, as he turned the corner to where his locker was, two sets of huge black hands grabbed Bart by his upper arms.

"HRRRRMMMFFFF!!!" Bart squealed as one pair of hands was meanly clamped over his mouth.

Bart struggled like a captured marine as he stood, trapped by a pair of huge, muscular black prison yard arms wrapped around his upper body and pinning his arms to his sides as another pair of huge hands quickly roped and roped and looped and roped his wrists in front of him.

How a stinking white sweat sock from his gym bag had wound up in his mouth as a gag, the handsome Bart Findley had no clue, it had happened too damned fast. He only knew that for whatever the fuck the reason, he was in a shit-load of trouble.

He was yanked to his sheer socked tip toes by the black man holding him in a vise-like grip and looked down with eyes opened wide in horror, watching as the other black man, a fucking skin-headed black man, went to work roping his most sexy sheer socked feet together, real tight.

"MMMMFFF," Bart sputtered helplessly, wriggling on his sheer socked toes as his feet were tied.

And then, a few moments later, Bart found himself being lugged between the two men and out the back door of the locker room, unseen and unheard by his buddy Travis, who was just a mere foot away, still getting dressed.

The bottoms of Bart's feet pointed at the ceiling as Jerome held him around his muscular upper body and Darren held him by his big, beefy socked calves. Then the two men literally carried Bart off to an awful fate.

"Fuck it, man, if we can't have the jock pussy himself, we'll just take the next best thing," Jerome said as he and Darren lugged Bart out the back door of the locker room.

Poor Bart had no idea what Jerome was talking about or why he had just been kidnapped. At first he thought it was just a mean joke being played on him by the team they'd just beat, but these two skinheads were *not* members of that team. Fuck, they weren't members of any team that Bart knew of. Clad in just his sexy boxer briefs and sheer silk socks with garters clipped to them, Bart screamed behind his sweat sock gag as Jerome and Darren tossed him into the back of a filthy van and quickly sped off with him.

Travis, totally unaware of what had befallen Bart, returned his thoughts and mind to the present. He watched on John's TV screen directly in front of him, feeling humiliated, as the video of his humiliation with the skinhead played over and over. Travis felt a mixture of rage, humiliation, and invasion of privacy as he repeatedly watched the video of himself licking the skin's boots and then sucking his cock.

"God, John, when is this going to stop?" Travis asked in anguish as John greased his hole.

John was silent, seeming to delight in what he was preparing Travis for this time.

"When are you going to stop blackmailing me, man?!" Travis

said. "How much more of this do you really and honestly think I can take?!"

In response, John reached forward and grinned at Travis as he hung his head, then scooped up a wad of Crisco and slopped it into Travis' face.

Travis gasped as the greasy Crisco hung from his forehead, nose and lips. He hung his head lower in humiliation and shame.

The smell of Travis' asshole was on John's fingers as he slapped the Crisco onto his face and now the smell sent his hard cock to pounding in his jockstrap.

"Does that answer your stupid question, O'Toole?" John asked as he resumed the task of greasing up the jock's hole.

He spread Crisco shortening over Travis' well-toned ass cheeks as he said, "There, now, you're pie-faced. That's another way you sports guys congratulate each other, by stupidly hitting each other in the face with cream pies. Har, har, har and har for you, O'Toole!"

Travis responded with a groan as John slapped and slathered the shortening over his ass mounds, giving those mounds some good, hard squeezes and twists at the same time.

Travis thought of how he had told his skinhead about this guy more than a week ago and he was still being blackmailed and used as a sex slave and a humiliation toy. And now, as his asshole and ass cheeks were being greased and fondled and prodded, he had to wonder just what John Broderick had in store for him this time out.

It had seemed like forever since the day that John had been able to videotape Travis and his skinhead in the deserted parking lot of the Calderfield College. And since that day, which had only been weeks ago, John had made it abundantly clear that he now owned Travis in every way possible. Whether it was just to have the handsomer than handsome jock tied up naked in his dorm room and seated on a big, fat butt-plug, or to do his college assignments, to force him to purchase men's designer clothing and jewelry for him at the Cherry Hill Mall, or to brutally rape him, John had made it very clear to Travis that with that video, he owned him lock stock and barrel, and until John had decreed otherwise, there would be no getting out of it for poor Travis.

As Travis watched himself on the TV screen licking the skinhead's boots, his cock throbbed big and hard in his jockstrap.

"Spike," Travis whispered.

As far as Travis could see (and feel) John was not going to be letting him off the tether on which he had so fiendishly balanced him. While tormenting, tying, and raping him, Travis had come to note how John seemed to delight in telling him how his ultra-successful and very rich dad would be *so* very ashamed and mortified to see his boy now.

While fucking Travis on his back, wearing nothing but a pair of sheer black dress socks with his trademark garters clipped to them, John would rail down at him over and over about how Travis' dad would be beyond livid if he could see his boy now with his sexy, muscular legs in the air; a college boy gripping his sheer socked ankles and getting his ass plowed. At times Travis wondered why John was so obsessed with his dad.

What Travis recalled most where his distinguished and handsome dad was concerned were the socks he'd always worn with his business attire. Even though Travis sometimes sported the Gold Toe brand of dress socks, it seemed that his dad had worn them all the time. Those Gold Toe brand socks having holes in the toes was what drove Travis out of his mind about his dad's socks. Many times Travis had asked his dad why, *why* he always had holes in the toes of his socks. It was always when his dad would come home after working all day at the bank and take his shoes off at the front door, seeing as Travis' mom did not want any muck or dirt tracked into the house. Travis' mom paid their cleaning lady an abundant salary (as far as his mom was concerned, that is) and she did not want any dirt from the outside marring her home. Travis' dad explained away his holey socks as just not taking care of them in the proper manner, but it was the day when Travis had turned eighteen years old, and had been accepted to Calderfield College, that he had discovered the real reason why most of his dad's dress socks were holey in the toes, and only his *black* Gold Toe brand socks at that.

On the day of his eighteenth birthday, Travis had received his acceptance letter to Calderfield College, and being that his dad had attended that same college, he wanted Travis Bradley O' Toole the third to be the first to know of his acceptance. So Travis got himself totally gussied up in a navy blue pinstriped suit by Calvin Klein, a white button down shirt by Hermes and a beautiful red silk power tie, one of his dad's (just for the occasion) by Hermes as well.

For his footwear, Travis helped himself to a pair of navy blue Gold Toe brand OTC socks from his dad's sock drawer, but made sure that there were no holes in the toes of the socks.

"Hmm, it's only his black socks by Gold Toe that always have holes in them," Travis said to himself as he sat on his Mom and Dad's bed and pulled the socks on and up to just under his knees. "I wonder why that is."

Travis completed his ensemble with a pair of his black wingtip shoes by Florsheim, tucked the acceptance letter from Calderfield College into his suit jacket pocket, then left the house and headed for his dad's Manhattan office.

As Travis entered the office building, he was filled with elation and a total feeling of pride. By the time he was in the elevator, he was beaming from ear to ear.

Travis got off on the fiftieth floor and, feeling like the newly appointed college student, happily walked up to the reception desk.

"Good afternoon, Mr. O' Toole," Maggie, his father's secretary, said as Travis stood before her desk.

"Hi Maggie, is my dad in?" Travis asked.

"He sure is. He has a couple of the junior executives in there with him, but I'm sure I don't need to announce you. He's always glad to see you, no matter how busy he is," Maggie said.

"Thanks Maggie," Travis said, and then walked down the short hallway toward his dad's private office.

When Travis reached the closed door to his dad's office, he extracted the envelope with the letter from Calderfield College from his suit jacket pocket, gripped it tight and slowly turned the doorknob. When the door was only slightly open, Travis heard his dad's voice, but did not understand what in all hell he was talking about.

"Fuck, never blindfolded me for this before, you feet and toe hungry mugs," his dad said.

Blindfolded? Toe hungry…*mugs?* Travis thought as he opened the door only slightly, for some reason he felt it best not to let his presence be known at the moment.

Travis peered through the crack and was shocked to see that his dad was sitting in his big executive chair with his feet up on his desk. But it was not seeing his dad with his feet up on his desk that had so unnerved him. Not only was his dad sitting with his feet up, but he was blindfolded with his own necktie and his shoes were not on his feet, just his black Gold Toe brand socks. Two of his junior executives, what his dad called his underlings, were methodically using office scissors to clip away sections of the gold material around his dad's black dress socks. Travis gulped hard at the sight of what was going on. Now he knew where the holes in his father's black dress socks came from. But the question that truly consumed the young Travis was, *Why? Why* was his dad allowing this? And in his office at that???

Travis stood rooted to the spot as he watched the two handsome junior executives snip away the gold material on his dad's dress socks, exposing a few of his toes, but most definitely his big toes on both feet.

The junior executives had pulled the gold material of the socks a bit up away from his dad's toes before they began snipping away at them, which sent massive chills through Travis' muscular being. As far as Travis was concerned, a man's socks were like his underpants, intimate and most private; they were not an article of clothing to be toyed with, unless in a private, sexual setting, that is. Travis, unnerved and disbelieving, stood as if rooted to the spot as the scene in front of him unfolded. Once a few toes, along with the big toes, of both feet were exposed at the fronts of his snipped socks, Travis' dad was then wallowing in what appeared to be sheer ecstasy behind his necktie/blindfold, as the two junior executives began sucking and slurping his exposed toes.

"Aw man, thanks for wearing your black Gold Toe dress socks today, Mr. O'Toole," one of the junior executives said in between slurping and sucking Travis' dad's toes on his right foot while holding super tight to the man's socked foot, almost holding it possessively.

"You're more than welcome, boys, but now, more sucking and less talking," Travis' dad said with a grin. "I allowed you to have your way with blindfolding me this time, *so I do expect* that you will both do your very best."

The two junior executives barked a hearty, "Yes Sir, Mr. O'Toole," as they went nuts sucking on the exposed toes of each of Travis' dad's feet, kneading his arches at the same time.

Travis simply stood there in disbelief. He leaned up against the wall next to the door of his dad's office and tried to sort out how he was feeling over this. What confused Travis the most was that his cock was hard and throbbing in his suit pants. What was it about seeing his dad in this position that had him so worked up in the crotch? Was it the fact that his no nonsense executive father had for whatever the fuck the reason relinquished control and power to these subordinates, or was it something deeper? Was it something in him that yearned for someone to somehow take control of him? Was seeing his dad this way somehow making Travis question his own sexuality and dominant nature? No, no, he was a jock, an All American straight dude. It was the power exchange that had somehow affected Travis' cock, that and nothing more, maybe.

When he was able to look into his dad's office again, the scene was still being played out. His dad was still blindfolded with his tie, and his socked feet were up on his desk as he leaned back in his chair with his two junior executives sucking and slurping his exposed toes through his snipped socks. What was different, however, was that Travis' dad was slowly stroking his cock, which was now sticking out of the fly of his suit trousers.

Holy shit, my dad's cock is out, Travis thought.

"Feels so damned good," Travis' dad panted. "You mugs were right, being blindfolded does make it feel all the more intense."

To Travis' further shock, the two junior executives weren't just sucking his dad's exposed toes, but they were also kissing those toes and the tops and bottoms of his socked feet as well.

Travis licked his lips and his hard cock throbbed in his pants. He was totally torn between simply leaving and staying till this scene was played out.

If he left, he knew that his dad's secretary would tell his dad that he had been there, so in a way he was trapped. He also knew that his dad would know that he had seen what was going on in the office. No, *Travis could not leave.* He knew that he would never reveal to his dad—or his mom, for that matter—what he had witnessed in the office, but he could not leave, that was for sure.

With that in mind, Travis took a deep breath and made a beeline to the men's room a few doors down the hall from where his dad's office was.

Upon entering the men's room, Travis was glad to see that he was the only one in there. He stuffed the envelope with the letter from Calderfield College into his suit jacket pocket, quickly dashed into a stall, closed and locked the door behind himself and stood in front of the toilet. Breathing heavily, he lowered the zipper on his suit pants, extracted his hard cock through the fly along with his testicles and took his manhood in hand. As visions of the two underlings sucking his dad's exposed toes coursed through his mind, all it took was a few good strokes to spew one of the biggest loads he could recall. Travis grunted and gasped in the men's room as thick wads of his sperm landed in the cold toilet water.

When he was done, Travis gave his balls a few good squeezes and the last droplets of his sperm erupted from his piss slit. With his head hanging down while he caught his breath, Travis did what most men have to do after having shot a big, hefty load, he pissed like a racehorse.

What was it about seeing those two junior executives sucking at his dad's toes that turned him on so much? He had just shot his load thinking of men working his dad in a degrading manner. He was a straight jock boy after all. Travis simply figured that it was seeing the power that his dad wielded over the two junior execs that had so engorged his cock, not the fact that they were male. Travis wondered if his dad had junior female executives under his command and if he made them suck his toes after they had clipped his Gold Toe socks. And what was up with all that anyway??? Why would those guys, or anyone for that matter, want to snip and cut at a guy's socks and then suck his toes?? Travis had heard of many kinds of kink and foot fetishes, but he had *never* heard of anything like this. The young future college student knew in his heart of hearts that he would *never* look at his dad's black Gold Toe brand socks the same way again.

A short while later, Travis packed himself back into his suit pants, exited the stall and washed his hands. He came out of the men's room feeling somewhat better and trekked back to his dad's office. This time when he got there, the door to his dad's office was wide open and his dad was standing behind the desk, his tie back around his neck where it belonged and signing some papers for the two junior executives who were standing in front of the desk. Travis instantly pasted a smile on his face and knocked on the open door to his dad's office.

"Travis, hey there, come on in, son," his dad said, gesturing at the same time for Travis to enter his office.

"Hey Dad, I just came to tell you some really awesome news, but if you're busy, or tied up at the moment," Travis said.

His comment wasn't lost on the two junior executives, who turned and looked rather lustfully at their boss's handsome offspring.

"Nah, no way, never too busy for you, Travis," his dad said. "And besides, Wagner and Broderick here were just leaving, weren't you, boys?"

The two junior executives said, "Yes Sir," took their signed papers and beat a hasty retreat from Travis' dad's office, smiling at Travis before closing the door behind them.

Broderick, Travis thought, the name sounding familiar. FUCK, one of the guys who worked for my dad was named Broderick, could it be John the blackmailer's dad???

But Travis could not think straight, or any other way at that moment, because John Broderick, the blackmailer who had sunk his jowls into the handsome college jock, was still busy slopping Travis' hole with Crisco shortening while stealing slurps and sucks on Travis' mussed hole; eating the shortening from back there and driving poor Travis crazy, which caused his huge cock to throb even more-so in his red jockstrap.

This day in John's dorm room was unlike most of the other days that Travis had come to spend there, the main difference being that it was right after a college football game, a game that Travis and his team had won with flying colors. After the cheering of the crowd, and having been carried off the field on Bart's shoulders, the champagne showers in the locker room and being hoisted by a few of his other football buddies and carried around the locker room on their shoulders and all the hoopla had died down and the victorious players stripped and headed for the showers was when John had made his appearance and given Travis the orders to be in his dorm room within the next fifteen minutes.

Without bothering to shower, Travis had pulled on a pair of jeans over his jockstrap, re-donned his football jersey and slipped his big sweat-socked feet into a pair of Nike trainers. Trembling in fear, anger and total rage, Travis made his way quickly through the campus and over to the building that housed John's dorm room.

Yes, this time in John's dorm room was very different, not so much in the ways that the jock boy would be totally humiliated and debased, but in his attire. Usually when Travis was made to come to John's dorm room for a "session," as it had come to be referred to, he was dressed to the nines either in a power suit or a blazer with slacks. On those occasions, Travis was always made to strip down to silk underpants and his trademark sheer dress socks and garters. But this time Travis was in his thick white football player sweat socks and a stinking jockstrap. This time John was getting his jollies humiliating the true jock side of Travis, rather than the well-dressed power-suited future executive.

But no matter his attire, Travis knew that this could not go on. Being blackmailed into sexual slavery was not how the handsome jock had planned on spending his free time at college. As his asshole was played with like it was a toy of sorts, Travis again whispered, *"Spike."*

2

An hour or so after greasing up Travis' asshole to the point that it was saturated with Crisco shortening, along with slathering the college jock's muscular butt cheeks with the shortening as well, John was once again doing to Travis Bradley O'Toole the fourth what he loved most, fucking him like the jock boy was some cheap whore.

"Fuck, you bastard, John, you lowlife scum," Travis said as he stood bent over the card table.

"Oh yeah, that's it O'Toole, swear at me, talk dirty for me, it drives me crazy all the more," John said with a laugh as he rammed his cock deep inside Travis.

With his legs spread as wide as possible, his gaping bunghole totally on display, Travis gripped the sides of the table tightly as John stood behind him, plowing in and out of his hole like a madman. John had stripped naked and Travis was now clad in just his long white sweat socks, his red jockstrap having been unceremoniously shucked off him by John a few seconds before the guy had ordered him to assume the position he was now in. As John fucked Travis hard with his steel-like erection, he slapped the football player's Crisco greased ass cheeks as well, the stinging sounds echoing in John's dorm room. The sound of squishing every time John entered the muscle boy's rectum was maddening to the jock. Travis felt beyond violated, beyond humiliated and beyond used and betrayed as he was fucked and fucked and fucked some more. Somehow this was worse than all that Spike had done or had done to him, because somewhere in his heart of hearts, Travis knew that Spike loved him; it was a strange and most unusual kind of love, but it was love nonetheless. Travis' erection stiffened to its full nine inches as he was fucked harder and harder by John. And as he was fucked, Travis thought of the sadistic sort of love that Spike had showered him with–even piss showered on him–and how it wasn't the same as John's style of cruelty. Travis also knew in his heart of hearts that Spike would not allow this atrocity to go on for much longer. Somehow Travis knew that Spike would put an end to John's blackmailing ways, but when??? When in all fucks would this end???

As John fucked Travis harder and harder, Travis held to the sides of the table as if his very life depended on it.

"Oh, you bastard, John. If you didn't have that damned video of me as leverage I would fucking beat you into dirt," Travis swore loudly.

"Ah, but that is so not going to happen you, jock pussy boy," John panted directly into Travis' ear, then sucked and bit his earlobe. "Because the original video is tucked away somewhere even a genius like you, or even your rich daddy, would never think to find it."

At the mention of his dad again, Travis knew that somehow this entire scenario *did* have something to do with his banker dad. *But what?*

"Fucking jock pussy," John muttered breathlessly as he shot his load into Travis' guts.

"Oh fuck, yeah, *fucking O'Toole hard!!"*

As he shot his load inside the handsome jock boy, John slapped and gripped Travis' greased up ass cheeks.

Travis grunted miserably, then to his embarrassment, shot his load directly under the table and onto his tall white sweat socks, his cock not even having been touched.

"Fuck, this is mortifying man!!" Travis swore breathlessly.

As he shot his load while John's load filled his rectum, Travis laid his head against the table and gripped the sides of it even tighter, his knuckles pronounced and glowing white. He cried miserably as he shot his load like a madman, heaving and panting in a mixture of ecstasy and shame. Over and over Travis said to himself, "I do not like this, I do not like this. *Oh God,* but then why did I just cum like gangbusters???"

When John and Travis were done shooting their loads, John let his spent and shriveled cock slip slowly out of the jock boy's asshole, one hand pressed hard against his fuck toy's ripped and muscular back, signaling him without speaking to keep himself splayed on the table. Slowly, John slid to his knees behind the fucked jock boy, spread his ass cheeks further and wallowed in a renewed ecstasy at the sight of Travis' cum sopped bunghole. John stuck out his tongue and buried his face in Travis' asshole. Travis swooned, grunted, sweated and swore as his asshole was eaten like it was a pussy. John greedily slurped and sucked his cum out of the jock's hole, seeming to be taking back what was rightfully his. As his hole was eaten and his ass cheeks were gripped tightly, Travis looked down and saw his own cum dripping down his white sweat socks. His cock tingled and his balls churned.

"Dad, what's the connection here???" Travis asked himself and knew that when he got back to his dorm room that he would have to do some investigating into John Broderick.

"Uhhhh, fuck," Travis shouted in pain as John stood up behind him and again buried his newly hard cock into the jock's asshole. "Holy shit!!!"

"That Viagra you got for me works wonders, jock pussy boy," John said through a laugh and began again thrusting in and out of Travis' warm, squishy hole. *"Damn, I could fuck you all day, O'Toole. Just eating this sweet pussy hole of yours got me all steely hard and nasty again!! And like I said, bud, I could fuck you all day, all fucking day."*

And that was just what John Broderick did that day; he fucked the star college football player, the golden boy, the coach's dream come true, Travis O'Toole the fourth.

After losing count of how many times he had been fucked that late afternoon, and after losing track of how much his asshole had not just been fucked but eaten and slobbered in like a pussy, Travis later found himself on his knees, blindfolded with a green bandanna and sucking and slurping on John's cock, tasting his own ass chowder on it.

"Fuck yeah, that feels awesome, O'Toole," John panted and gasped as Travis sucked his cock down to the root, feeling John's spent balls crashing against his chin. "Most guy's cocks are too sensitive after having cum as many times as I did today, but not me, man. I love having you suck and clean my cock with your mouth. "Yeah, like I said, if your rich daddy could see his boy now."

With that, John pissed long and hard into Travis' mouth, forcing the jock to swallow every drop of his sour tasting yellow stream.

Behind his blindfold, Travis rolled his eyes as he gulped down John's piss and ate his ass chowder off his cock as well.

"Oh yeah, drink my piss, you jock pussy boy," John said throatily. As John again called him by the name that Spike had dubbed him with, Travis grabbed his cock, which was again hard.

As he drank down the last of John's piss and resumed cleaning the guy's cock with his mouth and lips, Travis stroked a good load from himself.

John laughed mockingly and found himself thrusting in and out of Travis' mouth, ready to shoot a dry load or two as the blindfolded jock found himself then forced to suck, not just clean, his blackmailer's cock.

"Fuck, but how your mouth tightened around my pole when you shot your load, man, but that truck driver was right," John panted. "Jock pussy boy, you are."

A short while later, John held a blindfolded Travis by his upper arms and led him toward the open door of his dorm room, poor Travis shambling along for the ride.

"And out you go, jock pussy boy!" John shouted as he literally heaved the blindfolded Travis out of his dorm room by the hair, Travis still clad in just his tall white sweat socks.

"Hey!!! Holy shit," Travis reeled as he reached up to pull the green blindfold down to around his neck.

"And be ready to meet with me at the Zeller tuxedo shop at the mall tomorrow afternoon, O'Toole," John snapped as Travis stumbled, then regained his balance.

He looked up and down the hallway in naked shame.

"Tuxedo shop???" Travis roared back. "Why in all fucks do you need a tuxedo, of all things?"

"I have a date coming up with a really hot number who's taking me out for a show and dinner, and that date *is you*, O'Toole," John said with a laugh. "Tomorrow at two, in the tuxedo shop. Meet me here first and don't be late."

Standing alone in the hallway, naked but for his sweat socks, Travis caught his jeans, football jersey and sneakers as John tossed them out the door to him. As Travis stood there quickly pulling his jeans on, John slammed the door shut. He was done with Travis for that day; the jock boy had been used, abused, raped once again and dismissed. Once he was dressed and walking slowly—and in pain—out the main entrance of John's dorm, he tugged the green bandanna from his neck. Travis realized that John had kept his red jockstrap. Just another souvenir of his conquests, Travis thought miserably. As he passed slowly by a wastebasket, he tossed the green bandanna in.

"Fucking bastard, you are, John," Travis whispered to himself as he continued to walk slowly back to his dorm. "How can you do these things to a guy?? And why in hell *are you* doing these things to *me???*"

When Travis got back to his dorm room, he was glad that once again his roommate, Chad, was out, possibly in class. Travis didn't have any classes until the next morning, so he was glad that he would be able to rest up after the long day's festivities of having been the hero of the football game, and the awful and exhausting festivities of being abused and brutally raped once again in John's dorm room. Travis locked the door to his dorm room, angrily kicked his sneakers off his feet, shucked off his jeans, his football jersey, peeled his tall white cum crusted sweat socks from his feet and bounded into the bathroom to shower the sweat from football and sexual residue of the day off him.

As he showered, Travis soaped his muscular body vigorously, strongly, almost forcefully, trying to rid himself of the memories of what John Broderick had done to him yet again.

"Damn!" Travis swore as he bent over and spread his ass cheeks wide under the warm cascade of water.

Tears of agony and shame mixed with the water on Travis' handsome face as he watched John's cum drip from his asshole and sluice down the drain.

"*Spike,*" Travis whispered miserably, wondering why the skin hadn't yet taken care of the business of ridding him of being blackmailed.

Holding his ass cheeks wide in order to wash out his overused hole, Travis cried and sniveled miserably in a mixture of woe and outright rage.

When he was done showering, Travis dressed in a pair of dark blue silk boxer briefs by International Male with a matching tee shirt, a pair of blue jeans by Calvin Klein, a pull-over white polo shirt by Brooks Brothers; a pair of black leather flip-flops by Guess completed his casual look.

Once dressed and feeling somewhat better, Travis extracted his laptop from under his bed, fired it up and sat down with it at his desk.

"Okay, now lets see what I can find on you, my blackmailing buddy," Travis whispered as he brought up the Google search engine and typed in the name of the company his dad worked for and the name "Broderick" directly next to it.

Travis let out a throaty gasp when he saw the information that popped up in front of him. "Well, I'll fucking be."

"Shit, now it's all starting to make sense," Travis said as he read what was on the screen. "Dad, why didn't you ever tell me or mom about any of this? Or did you tell mom, but not me???"

Travis clicked on the article and read:

An assistant bank manager from New York City pleaded Not Guilty in federal court this past Thursday to embezzling more than fifty thousand dollars from First Time National Bank. Christian Broderick, forty-eight, worked at the New Brunswick branch of First Time National Bank when a routine nationwide audit this past March revealed that more than thirty thousand dollars was missing from transfers supposedly done by the office where Broderick was assistant manager. Evidence shows that from January 12th,

2009, to March 22, 2010, Broderick transferred small amounts of money, ranging from twenty dollars to six hundred dollars, to bank accounts belonging to him and family members. Broderick's direct supervisor, Bank Vice President Travis O'Toole the third commented, "I am deeply ashamed and embarrassed by the turn of events that occurred under my watch, and by someone I deeply trusted and enjoyed working with."

On one occasion it is alleged that Broderick transferred one thousand five hundred dollars to his personal account, according to the court records. He also fraudulently transferred money to make payments to his corporate credit card account, which included charges for personal expenses, according to bank sources. In total, Broderick allegedly embezzled fifty four thousand two hundred and fifty one dollars from the branch where he worked. The bank froze his account and recovered only four thousand eight hundred and seventy eight dollars. Broderick faces a maximum of thirty years in prison and will have to pay forty nine thousand three hundred and seventy two dollars in restitution. John Broderick, Christian Broderick's son, maintains that his father was set up to take the fall for his superiors at the bank, naming Travis O'Toole the third, saying that his father claims his supervisor set him up and that the missing money could no doubt be found in his secret accounts. Broderick's attorney, William Johnson, could not be reached immediately. Broderick denies any wrongdoing. A sentencing hearing is scheduled for ten AM, May third.

Travis sat back in his chair, re-read the article and whispered, "Holy shit."

3

It was an hour and a half or so after his capture in the Calderfield College locker room that hunky and handsome Bart Findley found out the true reason for his abduction.

Like all college football players, Bart knew the antics that could be played out between rival football teams. And Calderfield College was no different in this regard.

The dark haired, dark eyed suit wearing he-man had even staged some of those rivalry antics himself from time to time. From the traditional kidnapping of the winning team's mascot, to the capture and head-shaving of the rival team's captain, and even inking the bald head of the rival team's captain with the Calderfield College logo, Bart Findley had seen it all. (One time when he himself had manufactured the kidnapping of a football team's mascot, Bart had the joy of not only snagging their mascot, but shaving his head as well. Seeing as the winning college football team's mascot on that day was a real feminine dude dressed up like a leprechaun, and he had the longest, prettiest hair anyone had ever seen, Bart decided to shave the guy's head. Bart had managed to snatch the dude himself just before the winning team was set to leave Calderfield College in their rented bus. When the mascot was given back to them, his leprechaun costume was still pretty much intact, however, his pretty, long locks were gone and his head was shining bright as a new penny.)

But, at the tender age of twenty-one, heading for twenty-two in a few short weeks, nothing had ever prepared Bart Findley for what he now found himself enduring And what he was enduring was at the hands, fingers, tongues, mouths and cocks of eight black skinheads, including the two that had so easily abducted and *literally* carried him off from the Calderfield College locker room.

An hour and a half and ten minutes after his capture (to be exact) Bart Findley, golden boy of the Calderfield College Football team, found himself in the basement/locker room of a gym called Leo's Iron Man. The gym was not a state of the art facility like the one that the college boasted, nor was it the sort of upscale gym that was found at the now infamous Cherry Hill Mall. Rather, it was a dreary, musty scented, dimly lit gym, a place that would be frequented more by men looking for prison yard type workouts than well-dressed college jocks. When the van that Bart had been brought to the gym in stopped, he managed to heave his muscular self to his knees and look out the rear window.

"RRRMMFFF??" Bart reeled behind his sweat sock gag.

As he took in the sights of the rundown and burnt out buildings, Bart noted that he had been driven to a really seedy part of town.

He heard Jerome and Darren getting out of the front section of the van and then the van's front doors being slammed shut.

"The boys is going to love the hunky meat market we managed to snag for 'em all today," Bart heard Jerome say as they approached the back of the van, their big clonky boots pounding the pavement.

"Me, a meat market?" Bart asked himself, still kneeling there and looking at his tightly bound hands as he held them up in front of his tear-filled eyes.

Mustering up all the strength in his tongue that he could, Bart managed to spit out the sweat sock that had been crammed in his mouth. Just as the musty and awful tasting sock left his craw, the back doors of the van were pulled open.

At the sight of the two black skinheads grinning at him, Bart loudly ranted, "You thugs!!! What the hell is this all about??? Fuck, you guys have kidnapped me, for Christ's sake!!"

Leering meanly at their handsomer than handsome prize, the two skins reached forward into the van and meanly dragged Bart out by his upper arms.

"Fuckers, let go of me you guys!!! I swear, untie me and then we'll see if," Bart went on and on, but then he was silenced by two good clocks to his square jaw, one from Jerome and one from Darren. "HOOOFFFF!!!!"

"Now then, if you don't want to be chewin' on that stinky ole' sweat sock of yos again and if you don't want any of your pearly teeth knocked out, I would be keepin' my big yap shut from here on out, white boy," Jerome said with a laugh as he and Darren again lifted and lugged Bart between them, this time into the ratty looking building that housed the gym they had brought him to.

"M—meat market???" Bart whimpered softly, miserably and in pain, repeating what he'd heard earlier. "But I'm no faggot."

However, though, now it did seem that Bart Findley, the college football ace, *had* suddenly become the meat market for a group of overly muscular black skinheads, as they literally feasted and devoured at the handsome college jock's most tender and juicy parts.

"OH, AW, you skin-headed mangy mother fuckers!!! You thugs!!!" Bart roared upwards from where he was stretched out good, tight and taut and tied down on a bench in the man sweat scented downstairs locker room of Leo's Iron Man Gym.

Jerome and Darren had carried Bart down to the locker room amid the hoots and catcalls of the totally black population of men working out on free weights and weight training machines as well.

All the men who worked out at this gym were black, some were muscled to the point that Bart wondered if it was humanly possible to even be that big.

The handsome college football player was now lying on his muscular back, tied down at the feet, knees, thighs, waist and stomach; his robust chest was also rope twined beyond tight above and below his very delectable, pointy and huge man-sized nipples. Bart's muscular arms were pulled up and over his head and his wrists were tied down tight and unforgivingly to the bench he was lying on. The handsome football player was still wearing his classy looking navy blue OTC sheer socks, garters and matching silk boxer briefs.

"AW, you bastards, you guys can't be doing this to me!! This is a fucking *outrage!!"* Bart reeled manically, struggling in vain to get loose from the tight bonds. "This is a goddamned fucking outrage, I say!!!"

"Sorry to burst yo bubble, Mr. Football in his sexy sheer socks, garters and so pretty briefs, but *we is* doin' it to you, and we is gonna do it to you till you is good and chewed up and devoured and de-flowered at that, too," Jerome, Spike's buddy, a black muscular skinhead, said to Bart in between stealing sucks and slurps on one of the football player's pronounced nipples.

"YUH! GAWD," Bart seethed as Jerome slurped his nipple back into his mouth and sucked it hard between his thick lips. "You sons of bitches kidnapped me, holy shit!!'

"Yes Siree Mr. Football, kidnapped you most expertly, too," Darren said, laughing in between sucking the tied down football player's other nipple. "And none of yo football buddies was the wiser. Fuck, takin' you out that locker room was like the old fashioned shit o' takin' candy from a goddamned baby."

Bart lifted his head from the bench and watched in a state of disbelief as Jerome and Darren feasted like two wild men on his nipples. Two other black skinheads, Darnell and Malik, took turns sucking at Bart's big balls, which they had extracted from his silk boxer briefs through the fly. Above him, Bart could feel two other skinheads, their names Willie and Reginald, as their long tongues slathered and sucked and licked and slobbered at the tied down jock's exposed hairy, stinky armpits, and lastly, at his big size twelve sheer socked feet. Two black skinheads named Jamal and Maurice were in a state of ecstasy as they crooned over and licked, sucked, kissed and slobbered over the captive football player's sexily dressed feet, his arches, his toes and the bottoms and tops of his tied down tootsies. All the black skinheads feasting on the college football player were nude except for sneakers, sweat socks and steely looking erections between their muscular legs.

Bart had once been told of a college football rivalry where a hero football player had been very cleverly abducted and left tied up and blindfolded to a bed in a female sorority house. When the football player's blindfold had been removed, he was forced to lie on the bed in total bondage while his muscular body, his cock, and mouth were all used to service some of the evil girlfriends of the rival football team that his team had bested earlier that day. When the bitches had finally released the football player, he was one very exhausted but also happy dude. Of course, this was just an urban legend, there was nothing substantial to back it up, but Bart had to admit that when he had heard about it, he was furiously jealous of the kidnapped football player. The thought of being used and sexually abused by a group of horned up sexy bitches was just too much for the young jock to contemplate without a hard-on the size of a flagpole. But to be used in the way the eight black skinheads were presently using and abusing him, well, in the captured jock's opinion, this was not one for the history books or for urban legends, for that matter.

"Wh—what's the fucking point of all this, dudes?" Bart reeled as his cock strummed in fear like a thing alive in his thin silk underpants, making a most erotic looking outline.

Bart was breathless as he was voraciously feasted on at the nipples, testicles, armpits and his feet. Fingers tugged at his soggy armpit hair and hands were squeezing his big socked feet as well. The football player had definitely become the meat market for these twisted skinheads. While being mauled, chewed on and feasted on Bart wondered what the other guys working out upstairs in the gym might do to him as well once these eight were done with him, that is if they got done with him. The way they were literally devouring him, it seemed to the football player like there wouldn't be much left of him whatsoever when this was over.

"The point, Mr. Football, is, being that we couldn't snag yo bud, the jock pussy boy, 'cause Spike won't allow it no mo, we decided to took the next best thing, *you,*" Jerome said with a grin, his pearly white teeth and one gold tooth gleaming. He twisted and kneaded the jock's swollen nipple between his fingers and thumb as he spoke. "So it's like if Miss America can't fulfill her duties, the first runner up *has* to fill in, or in yo case, *be* filled in!"

"WH—WHA, who in all fucks is the jock pussy boy, what in all hell is a jock pussy boy, and *who* in all hell is Spike?" Bart fumed, his handsome head rising as he spoke through clenched teeth.

Jerome snickered meanly as Willie reached forward from where he was licking one of Bart's armpits and pushed the football player's head back down on the bench with a meaty sized hand over his forehead.

"Relax dude," Willie said as Bart again looked straight up at the ceiling of the dingy and musty scented locker room. "You is doin' fine...HAR!!!"

As the sucking and slurping and feasting at his most private parts went on, Jerome again smiled evilly at their captured prize and said, "Yo don't know him as the jock pussy boy, yo and all yo other suit buddies call him Travis. And Spike, well, that be yo Travis' BF, his boy-friend."

At the sound of Jerome's words, Bart's head again sprang up from the bench he was tied to as if from a springboard.

"WHAAATTT?" Bart seethed at Jerome as the man leaned down and resumed sucking hard at his nipple. "Yuuuuuuhhh, fucker, my buddy Travis, the BF of a skinhead dude??? Shit, you guys are all deranged and...HHHHRRRRRMMMFFFFFF!!!"

But then, Bart's words were cut short as his head was again pushed down to the bench, this time by the black muscled skinhead named Willie. Willie did not resume licking at Bart's armpit, instead he fed the unwilling jock his huge ten inches of pure man-meat.

"HHHHRRRMMMFFF!!!" Bart screamed even more, now in disbelief, as he was suddenly initiated into the art of cock sucking. "GGGRRFFFF..."

"Yeah, that's it, Mr. Football, suck my huge cock. Lickin' all the crud and mess outa those pits of yours and smellin' all that manliness in them pits has got me all worked up like yo can't believe." Willie sneered down at Bart and slid his cock in and out of the trapped jock's mouth.

Bart felt as if his jaws were being stretched past their limits. Even in the locker room after a game, when all the players were getting themselves stripped down before heading for the showers, he'd never seen such a piece of man-meat. And now he was being forced to chow down on one.

Bart looked upward as his eyes crossed and saw that the gigantically muscular black skinhead named Willie was standing directly over him, straddling the bench. He slid his cock in, then halfway out, and then back in the jock's mouth. The way that Willie was feeding Bart his huge cock caused his kiwi-sized balls to land on Bart's nose each time, treating the football player to a hearty sniff of his sweaty nuts.

"Yeah, that's it, Mr. Football, get a good rhythm goin' wit dat mouth o' yo's," Willie panted as Bart was forced to do his bidding.

To Bart, Willie's cock tasted as if the remnants of pussy juice were all over it. The football player wondered how long ago it was that this guy had fucked some woman, and now was being serviced again, this time by a sheer socked, well-dressed captured college football dude at that. Oh, but for the injustice of it all.

"HHHRRRMMMFFFF," Bart squealed as Willie's cock slid down his throat, nearly choking him.

"Yeah, eat my cock, you handsome dude," Willie crooned down at Bart and then meanly spit in his eyes.

The other black skinhead who had been licking at Bart's armpits stood up and took position next to Willie.

"I go next, Willie," Reginald said demandingly, his huge cock hard as steel and ready for some servicing.

"Oh yes, *yes,* Reg, all us goin' to feed Mr. Football our sperm offerings," Willie said as tears trickled down Bart's face.

At Bart's crotch area Darnell and Malik, two nearly six feet tall black skinheads *who had* actually met in prison, had licked and sucked and chewed the jock's testicles up to twice their size. Unbeknownst to the captive jock, torturing a guy's testicles with their tongues and mouths was their specialty. The two skinheads had had many a good time while in prison, snagging the white prisoners and licking and tonguing their balls. Bart grunted and groaned in pain every time his testicles were tortured orally by the two thugs. In his sexy boxer briefs, Bart's erect cock throbbed with fear. Every time he grunted and groaned in pain, it was a vibrating rhythm around Willie's cock as it speared the football player's mouth.

"MMM, best tastin' white boy nuts I ate in a long while," Darnell commented meanly. "We never roasted nuts like this back in prison."

"RRRRMMMFFF," Bart blubbered at hearing what Darnell had just said, tears streaming from his beautiful eyes.

But then, as Darnell sucked and chomped on the jock's testicles, sticking out of his sheer boxer briefs, he was not able to look down to see, but he felt Malik's fingers roaming into his underpants and bringing out his terror-filled, hard cock. Malik squatted down next to his buddy, Darnell.

As Darnell worked over Bart's balls in a mean and pressurized manner with his mouth and tongue, Malik opened wide and gobbled Bart's man-meat into his hungry craw.

"RRRRMMMFFF," Bart wailed in a mixture of forced ecstasy and rage as it was now Reginald's cock that was spearing his mouth, then it was Willie's again, then Reginald's.

It seemed that the two men were having some sort of sick and twisted contest to see who would feed the jock their cum first.

At Bart's navy blue sheer socked feet, Jamal and Maurice, two heavy duty foot fetishists, were having the time of their lives with the jock's well-dressed tootsies.

"Aw man, Stacy Adams socks, I know these stinkers anywhere," Jamal, a lanky, well-toned skinhead said as he heartily sniffed the bottoms of Bart's delectable, well-shaped feet. "Just 'cause I a skin don't mean I don't know classy footwear when I sees it, *and* smell and taste it, too, fuckin' pretty football player in sheer socks we got here; and garters, too, how hot is that? Just wish his feet stank a bit more, though."

"Well, Jerome and Darren caught this jock boy *after* he had showered the stink off him," Maurice, a husky black skinhead, said with a chuckle as he sniffed and licked the bottom of Bart's other foot. "But no way I'm sayin' no to these feets of his. Socks so sheer I can see the goddamned outlines on the bottoms of these big football feet of his."

The two skinheads at Bart's sheer socked feet gloated meanly, snapped his elastic garters against his skin and licked and sucked at the jock's sheer socked toes.

And so, as Bart lay atop the bench like a cheap whore at a sexual buffet in the musty and dim locker room, he cried miserably. It wasn't long before the studly and very manly jock was swallowing his first load of black skinhead cum, courtesy of Willie.

"RRRMMMFFFFF!!!" Bart thundered in incredulousness as Willie's thick, milky sperm erupted from his cock and began its way down the trapped football player's throat. "GGGRRRMMMFFFF!!!"

"Yeah, that's it, white boy, eat my goddamned spunk," Willie ordered. As Bart sputtered, remnants of Willie's cum seeped from the sides of the football player's trembling mouth. "Fucking white boy, big as you are for a football dude, yo mouth ain't no way big enough to house my spurtin' manhood. Damn!!!"

Willie cupped his big balls in hand, squeezed them and more gooey mess erupted from his huge cock, overflowing into Bart's mouth. "GGGRRRRRFFFFF." Bart choked on the heavy load, his eyes squeezing shut as he tasted Willie's sperm, swallowed and felt what he could not swallow trickling down the sides of his wide open jaws.

As Willie seemed to endlessly cum, the other black skinheads continued feasting on Bart's tits and feet.

"OOOOOOHHH fuck, fuck yeah, sweet football player dee-lite," Willie crooned as he went on and on, feeding Bart his sperm as the football player cried.

When Willie was finally done shooting his load, Bart's lips were caked up with crusted sperm. The second Willie's cock was out of the jock's mouth, he roared, "You fucking skinhead lowlife, you'll pay f—!" but Bart's words were cut off as Reginald quickly slid his hard black man meat into the football player's quivering mouth.

"RRRMMMMFFF!!!" Bart squealed as he thought to himself, Oh fuck, I'm sucking another cock here!

"OOO yeah, football-dee-lite's mouth feels like velvet after yo filled it with yo spunk, Willie!" Reginald laughed and gasped as he slid his cock in and out of Bart's mouth.

Willie smiled evilly and settled down at Bart's hairy, sweaty and saliva soaked armpits. While his cock rejuvenated itself, Willie busied himself licking and slurping at the captive football hunk's armpit.

As Reginald now fucked his mouth, Bart's eyes opened wide in sheer terror as he saw all the other black skinheads now lined up with their cocks sticking straight out, hard as steel, and their cum-filled balls hanging low between their tree-trunk-like legs.

"RRRRMMMMMFFF!!! HHRRRMMMF FFF," Bart cried pitifully at the degradation as he sucked the second cock of his life knowing that before this was over, he would have sucked eight cocks, and no doubt swallowed all the cum from those cocks as well.

To further Bart's dismay, he saw that even Willie was in line to have his cock sucked *again,* and even though he had just fed the football player a huge helping of his sperm, it looked like the guy was hard enough to feed him another huge helping. From above the bench he was laying on, Bart could hear heavy weights being dropped to the floor. Again, he wondered what the other men in the gym would do to him once these lowlifes were done.

"AWWW, mother fucker," Reginald grunted as his eyes crossed and he began spurting his mess into Bart's unwilling mouth. "Squeeze those jowls of yours around my man-meat, white boy. Make that mouth of yo's feel like the goddamned pussy hole we done made it into today."

Bart did as he was told and squeezed his jaws tight around Reginald's spurting cock, all the while looking up at the skinhead with eyes opened wide in terror.

"OOOOO yeah, fucking A, white boy, that feels right nice," Reginald said.

When Bart heard Jerome say to his buddy Darren, "Looks like this white boy is learning the art of cock suckin' even faster than his jock pussy boy buddy, Travis, did," Bart knew that he and Travis would have a lot to talk about *if* he ever got out of this mess.

But then, once again, Bart's thoughts were cut short as he finished swallowing Reginald's sour tasting spunk. Before he could utter a word, Reginald extracted his cock slowly from his mouth. Now it was Jerome's turn at having his cock sucked. Jerome grunted throatily as he slid his huge hard and throbbing black cock into the football jock's mouth.

Bart cried louder now as his mouth was again filled with cock.

Jerome fucked Bart's mouth, shot his load, made Bart swallow it, and then it was Malik's turn, followed by Jamal, followed by Willie again.

By the time all eight of the skinheads had forced Bart to suck them off and swallow their loads, Bart was a sputtering and crying like an enraged mess of a football player.

"B—bastards, goddamned thugs, my mouth feels stretched longer than a worn out silk sock," Bart shrilled upwards at his tormentors. "How could you dudes do this to me???"

"Oh, shut yo yap, white boy," Willie said as he slid his flaccid cock into Bart's mouth. "*Oh man,* every time I cum like I just did I always has to piss like a goddamned racehorse."

And with that, Willie unleashed a torrent of yellow, sour tasting piss into Bart's mouth.

"OOOOOOOHHHFFFF," Bart screamed once again in disbelief as now he was forced to drink piss.

"Now, you be our human toilet, football dee-lite," Willie said, then laughed and forced Bart to chow down on his warm lemonade as it cascaded in torrents from his big, flaccid cock.

4

It was the day after the Calderfield College's football victory, which was also the day after one of Travis O' Toole's the fourth's fateful sessions in John the blackmailer's dorm room. The handsome jock awoke with his asshole in searing pain despite all the warm water and suds he had subjected it to when he had showered and washed it out the afternoon before. When Travis had gotten back to his dorm room all he had done was showered, learned about the case against John Broderick's dad for embezzlement and then hit the hay, as the saying went. The jock, despite the fact that he was exhausted and ravenously hungry after having just played a grueling game of football and then been used for hours as a sex toy, could not fathom eating a thing. Thinking that after what John had literally done, raping the tar out of him, he would simply vomit out anything he would have eaten. Unbelievable as it was to himself, despite the pain in one of his most private areas, he had slept through the night.

And not only had he slept through the night, but he had also dreamed of his skinhead, Spike. Considering what John had been putting him through on an almost daily basis these last few weeks, it was not surprising that he had dreamt of Spike. But now Travis wondered if somehow John was seeking revenge for his dad through him, seeing as it was Travis' dad who had implicated the man in the case against him. As Travis lay there and the cobwebs of sleep departed, he crossed his hands behind his head and recalled the dream he had just had starring Spike. Actually, it was more a memory, something that had happened shortly after Spike had taken his jock pussy boy for the totally balding haircut at the old fashioned barber shop run by Gus, the Italian accented barber at the Cherry Hill Mall.

Spike's Journal

Ha, the afternoon after my jock pussy boy's fatal haircut by my barber buddy, Gus, the pretty jock had met up with his buddy Bart and the other suit men in a classy café near the college campus for espresso and a light snack, no hard liquor or beer for those prissy boys, let me tell you. Him and his buds had no idea that I was there, spying on them, you might say. I had set myself up at a back corner table and made sure not to smoke, didn't want to give myself away. I was there to find out what the jock pussy had to say about the latest goings on in his pathetic life, ha, a life that I was spicing up for him by leaps and bounds, you could say. The jock pussy boy's buddies complimented him–*they actually complimented him*–on his new look, and even some of the women in his classes said he looked absolutely awesome, sort of like a marine or a soldier, HA! Right, some marine or soldier that jock pussy would make, a total submissive he is, *my* total submissive.

Despite the compliments, I know that the jock pussy hated his new look; he hated the barber who had shorn away his designer haircut; he hated the barber for what he had done to him after cutting and shaving off all his hair with my permission, that was. Returning to his dorm room after having hung out with the suit men, he slammed the door to his room and stomped in. He would come to realize that despite it all, that he *did not* hate me, I can only assume that the question that burned through the jock pussy's very being was, *why???* Why didn't he hate me? I didn't need a crystal fucking ball to see that the jock pussy was suffering through the trials and tribulations I had put him through. I had literally demoralized him, humiliated him, allowed him to be viciously raped, and forced him into sexual servitude. Fuck, I had even taken so much of his fine clothing from him. I had forced him to purchase new boots for me (for him to worship, nonetheless). Damn, and it was those cruddy boots of mine that I wore on a daily basis that had so hypnotized and mesmerized the handsome well-dressed jock pussy. No, in his heart of fucking hearts, the jock pussy had to know that he did not hate me. Fuck, he wouldn't keep coming back for more of me and my boots if he hated me. He feared me, and yet that fear translated into his cock engorging to a full nine inch erection. And if that was the case, *how* could he hate me?

On that day, my jock pussy had the dorm room all to himself. He had already hung out all bald and suited with his suited buddies in the classy café. His roommate, a muscle boy named Chad Towers, had afternoon classes, which left the jock pussy alone with some privacy to study or just sit and brood and sulk as he lifted and heaved a men's designer leather bag across the room.

I was already outside the jock pussy's dorm room when I heard him shout, "Damn!!!" as he took in his bald reflection in a mirror. Ha!!!

As I stood in front of his dorm room door, I could just imagine jock pussy changing into something like a pair of sheer–fuck, just about see-through–tight pink silk briefs by 2X1ST and a pair of light blue OTC sheer thick and fucking thin socks by Stacy Adams, along with matching light blue garters clipped to them; those garters, as the jock pussy told me eventually, had been a gift to him from his buddy Bart. The light blue thick and thin socks had contrasted real nicely with the dark blue suit that the jock pussy had worn that day to classes and then to the café for espresso and a light snack. But now was not the time for silk briefs or silk fucking socks, my jock pussy thought. Now it was time for white cotton boxer briefs and thick white sweat socks, because now the jock pussy had decided that it was time for the gym and his workout.

But I had other plans in mind for him at that moment and knocked on the door, ha!

The jock pussy called out, "Who is it?" as if he was almost afraid of who it could be.

"It's your Master Skin, jock pussy boy. Open the fucking door now and be fucking *quick* about it, or I'll make you sorrier than you already are!"

The jock pussy's lips were suddenly trembling as he called out, "S—Sir??" I could only imagine that he was wondering how the fuck I had gotten into the building. Well, I let him wonder because I have my ways.

"Yeah, it's your Master, your *Sir*, now open this door, jock pussy, and don't make me say it again, *got it?*" I said and I was sure that he could smell my cigarette smoke.

Ha, I was smoking in the hallway, in a non-fucking-smoking hallway at that. If anyone reported me, the jock pussy would be done for.

"Uh, yes, Sir, I'll uh, I'll be right there Spi—er—Sir," he called out and I knew for a fact that he was reaching for his suit pants, it was just his nature. "I, uh, I just have to put on my pants and shirt and—"

"*Fuck that shit,* jock pussy, you know I don't give a fuck if you're naked or in your silk socks, or whatever," I jeered from behind the door and banged again, harder this time. "Open this fucking door now or I'll set my black skinhead buds on you again!"

I heard the fucking jock pussy gulp and then he padded quickly to the door, no doubt on silk socked feet. He opened the door. I blew smoke in his face and trudged in, eyeing him cruelly and lustfully when I saw how he was so scantily clothed. What a sight he was, let me tell you, buds. The jock pussy quickly shut and locked the door behind me. At the sight of me in my ratty sweat stained tee shirt, worn jeans and black work boots, the jock pussy's cock began engorging in his tight silk briefs, betraying him. God, I loved the effect I had on him. He was mine, and would be for the rest of our lives.

"S—sorry Sir, I wasn't thinking when you asked me to open," the jock pussy began, but I quickly cut his words off, backhanding him good and fucking hard across his handsome face.

"I don't recall granting you permission to speak, jock pussy," I spat at him, literally.

A second later, my jock pussy found himself on the floor on his hands and knees and staring at the grungy black work boots I was wearing.

"Next time you'll move faster, won't you, you waste of a man, you waste of a cock, you jock pussy," I said from above as I towered over the trembling and lip quivering jock pussy. "Speak!!!!"

"Y—yes, Sir, yes," he replied, obviously still feeling disbelief over the fact that a seeming lowlife like me was in his dorm room.

It was bad enough that my torments and antics had taken place with him at the Cherry Hill Mall, but I was sure at that moment that he was thinking what in all hell did I plan to do with him *here,* in his dorm room of all places?

And I was also sure he was wondering why the fuck he didn't deck me just then, his hands curling into big meaty fists attested to that. Boy could I read his body language or what? He was twice my size, after all, and he could flatten me in a heartbeat *if* he chose to. *But* he didn't choose to. He was in awe of me and I know that he was wondering why in all hell he allowed me to beat on him, to humiliate him, to use him in the ways that I had come to.

"Fuck me man, look at you, *just look at you,* in fucking silky pink briefs and of course your silk socks and garters, jeez," I railed down at my beautiful prize, hacked up a good mouthful of saliva, then spit directly down onto the jock pussy's head. "Fucking total waste of a man, you are."

As my spit slithered over his head, the jock pussy whimpered miserably.

Tears rose in his eyes and he clenched his teeth.

Then, without my permission being granted, he grabbed the front of one of my grungy boots, leaned down even further from his kneeling position and kissed the boot hard, his tears landing on it. He then licked up the tears as he kissed my boot again and again.

"Looks like I showed up at the right fucking time, huh jock pussy?" I asked.

I meanly pulled my boot away and out of his grip, then dropped the butt of my cigarette on the floor in front of the football jock. The jock pussy bowed his head and watched as I ground out the cigarette under the heel of one of my boots.

"Now do what the fuck I taught you to do with that cigarette butt, jock pussy!" I demanded.

Without looking up, he picked up the cigarette butt from the floor, gobbled it into his mouth and chewed.

I laughed voraciously, then reached down and slapped my jock pussy hard across his bald head.

After he swallowed my rancid tasting cigarette butt, he slowly looked up at me, the man who had invaded his life and somehow seduced and, *yes,* enslaved him.

"Sir, permission to speak, please?" the jock pussy warbled and saw my erection tenting my jeans, just as his was now tenting his tight silk briefs.

"Nah, jock pussy, I got somethin' else in mind for you at the moment rather than listening to you prattle," I said, then laughed and shucked a designer backpack off my back, just another gift that I had made my jock pussy buy for me on one of our shopping excursions at the Cherry Hill Mall. "So keep that yap shut, got it?"

The jock pussy nodded when he saw me extract a few lengths of white rope and a sweat soaked red bandanna from my backpack.

A few moments later, my prize found himself lying on his bed on his stomach with his hands roped at the wrists to the head-board and silk socked and gartered feet lashed to the footboard. I had taken my damned sweet time binding the jock pussy's silk socked feet to the footboard, seeing as I loved handling and massaging those feet of his as I did so. As his socked feet were handled and tied, the jock pussy's erection pounded hard in his pink silk briefs. I had filled his sensuous mouth with my stinking and rancid sweat soaked red bandanna, along with a rope tied over it, jamming it in place. I can't say just how very amazing and sexy and helpless he looked tied up the way I now had him, and fuck, it made me fall even more head over boot heels in love with him, ha!

Seconds later, the jock pussy boy was whimpering miserably behind the bandanna gag, while behind him I methodically snipped away the back section of the jock pussy boy's silk briefs with a pair of razor-sharp workman's scissors that I had also had in my backpack.

"MMMMFFFF," the jock pussy murmured pitifully. Each time he swallowed he was treated to a mouth and throat-full of the sweat and body odor that had accumulated on the bandanna that I had effectively gagged him with.

"Relax jock pussy boy, I won't let any harm come to ya," I said tauntingly and dropped the shreds of his underpants on the floor. "I just felt like coming over here and checking on your bald head and to work ya over a bit, too. HAR, HAR, HAR."

The jock pussy looked over at me, and again the sight of his beautiful tear-filled eyes almost broke my fucking heart. Seeing the gloriously muscular and handsome jock tied up the way I had him in his newly torn up briefs and his signature silk socks and garters made my heart skip a few beats. It still amazed me at times, especially at moments like this, when I had him totally under my control, that this fucking beautiful specimen of a guy was mine, and would always be mine. I would make sure of it. Much as I enjoyed pussy and a pair of nice girlie tits, I had to fucking admit that this fucking guy, this well-dressed jock pussy boy, had totally overwhelmed me. I had never seen a guy as pretty and yes, submissive, as the jock pussy. From the moment I laid eyes on him at the Cherry Hill Mall, I knew that I had to make the jock boy mine. And so far, I had done it, and I would continue to do it.

As my jock pussy boy lay tied to his bed and gagged, I reached into the pocket of my jeans and extracted a handful of quarters.

"I went to the change machine in the laundry room to get these," I said, jingling the quarters in my hands.

"Mmmmfff?" the jock pussy asked as his eyes rolled back.

"I figured you were wondering why I lashed ya to you your bed and gagged ya like that," I said, chuckling meanly. "Actually, I tied you up just because I can, okay jock pussy?"

At that, the handsome angel looked at me again and simply nodded. I had all to do to keep myself from belly laughing at him. Man, he was mine, all mine.

"Well, it's actually quite simple why I tied and gagged you this way, *my* jock pussy. A few buddies of mine saw you recently with your new baldy look and they loved it. They said I had made you look like a marine, a fucking jarhead, a leatherneck, and damn!!! One of 'em saw you when you were workin' out at the gym at the Cherry Hill Mall. You were wearin' a pair of really tight fitting gym shorts and my buddy said that you had an ass tight enough to bounce quarters off of. I totally told him that he was wrong, but he insisted, jock pussy. So I'm here to find out if he was right about that ass of yours."

The jock pussy groaned miserably as I slid a pillow under his crotch, elevating his butt globes.

Then, he screamed out in pain behind the bandanna gag as I took up position next to him, raised my hand high and slammed a quarter down hard on one of his butt cheeks. It made a sort of sound like a splat and the jock pussy groaned miserably.

"Damn, check it out, your ass *is* so tight and well-formed that quarters *do* bounce off it, jock pussy," I said with a laugh as I slammed another quarter down on his butt globes.

I watched in a state of awe as the side of the quarter connected hard with the jock pussy's ass cheek, bounced almost as high as the fucking ceiling and then landed on the floor.

My jock pussy squealed as I bounced quarter after quarter off his upturned and very paramount butt cheeks. The crack of his ass looked like the crack of a pussy to me, ha!

"Nice way to redden a jock's butt cheeks, huh pussy?" I asked him and slammed another two quarters down on his ass cheeks in quick succession.

Again he squealed miserably, but damn, his cock was hard as steel and dripping pre-cum. If the jock pussy could have replied to my question, I was sure he would have said, "If it makes you happy to redden my ass in this manner, then it makes me happy as well, Sir."

After awhile, the sounds of quarters being bounced off the jock pussy's butt cheeks and then landing on the floor became maddening for my tied up jock. He began to squirm and groan miserably.

When I ran out of quarters, I collected them from the floor and began a second round of bouncing them off my jock pussy's ass cheeks. Again he screamed and screamed and now beautiful tears flowed every time I slammed a quarter against his behind.

By the time I got to the third and fourth rounds of my sadistic game, the jock's bottom looked like a mess of scratches, welts and pelt marks.

"There, now ya got an ass worthy of me, jock pussy," I growled, then bounced a few last quarters off his butt cheeks just to torment the guy a bit more and to make sure he knew who the boss was.

"RRRMMMMMFFF!!!" he screamed in reply.

"Maybe at some point I'll take ya to a tattoo place and have our names tattooed on those ass cheeks of yours, what do you think, jock pussy?" I asked him, them, in a few quick motions, I had the rope over the bandanna gag undone and took the bandanna out of his mouth.

"Speak, jock pussy!" I demanded and then slid a finger deep into his rectal hole.

He gasped before saying, "Sir, if it would make you happy to tattoo your name and mine on my ass cheeks, then it would make me happy as well, Sir."

I grinned lecherously and said, "Damn, I've trained you better than good, huh jock pussy? Speak!"

"Sir, yes Sir, I am totally trained, Sir," he said heartily.

"Now then, how about after I untie you, you pay me a little lip service with a blowjob and then show me the dorm where that fucker John lives?"

The jock pussy leaned forward, and without permission, kissed my cheek.

5

And so, on this morning, after having spent time with John yet again, the jock was not only in searing pain in his rectum, but he was also voraciously hungry. As he chucked the sheets off him and sat up in bed wiping the sleep dust out of his gloriously beautiful eyes, Travis figured he would stop at the gourmet deli on campus before heading for his first class of the day.

As Travis climbed out of bed, clad in just a pair of tight white cotton boxer briefs by International Male, he heard a knock on his bedroom door.

"Yeah, uh, who is it?" Travis called out, noting how his nine inch piss filled erection was tenting his tight fitting boxer briefs real sexily.

"Hey there bud, it's your faithful roomie, Chad," his roommate said. "Just wanted to let you know that the bathroom is free if you need it. And I made us a fresh pot of coffee out here as well, bud."

"Oh, uh, cool, thanks Chad," Travis called back.

As he stood there naked but for his white boxer briefs, the door to his bedroom opened and there stood his handsome roommate, Chad Towers. The name fitting him perfectly, seeing as the black haired, dark eyed twenty-two year old Chad Towers, son of Michael Towers, the jewelry company owner, was better than six feet, two inches tall.

Standing in the archway of Travis' bedroom door, dressed in blue jeans by Ralph Lauren, a pull-over orange polo shirt with the Ralph

Lauren monogram on the left breast and fashionable ankle length black dress boots by Kenneth Cole, Travis' roommate struck an imposing sort of pose. He took in the sight of Travis in just his boxer briefs and piss filled erection and grinned from ear to ear. Not only was chad Towers better than six feet tall, but he was well toned and muscular, seeing as he worked out every day at the gym in The Cherry Hill Mall. He called his body "Body by Chad" and planned to one day own his own string of gyms. Unlike Travis, he did not intend to follow in his father's footsteps.

Chad had an eight pack stomach, arms so muscled that they looked like knotted cables, shoulders as wide as a doorway and hands the size of hams. Actually, his hands were big enough to punch holes through walls if the avid bodybuilder decided to do so, that is.

His jet black hair was cut in the style of an old-fashioned Marcello, which set off his steely features and chiseled jawline exquisitely. It also added some contrast to his build, giving him a bit of a geeky look, for lack of a better word.

"That was some game yesterday, O'Toole," Chad said, still grinning at the sight of his vulnerable looking roommate standing there in just his boxer briefs, his erection now dripping beads of piss, seeing as Travis had to piss like a racehorse at that point.

"Yeah, it was pretty hefty, huh, Chad?" Travis replied, a grin forming on his handsome face as well. "I, uh, didn't see you in the bleachers though, bud."

"Oh, I was there, O'Toole, I wouldn't have missed it for the world. I just love college rival football games," Chad said as he stepped close to his roommate, clapping Travis hard on the shoulder. "I loved being witness to that winning touchdown you scored for us, bud. It made me proud to be your roommate. I'll bet after Bart Findley carried you on his shoulders to the locker room you and all your suited buddies went out and got rip roaring drunk, huh?"

Travis smiled almost woefully, too embarrassed, totally mortified, and too bitter to actually tell Chad how he had spent his time after the game. The bitterest reminder of the day before was how his asshole twitched every time he moved.

"Uh, no, not really, I, uh, didn't go out, although I think Bart and the other suit men did. I just came back here after a while and conked out, I was really tired, and I had no classes," Travis explained, tripping stupidly over his words.

"Yeah, right," Chad chuckled, and again clapped Travis hard on the shoulder. "Knowing you and those suited buds of yours, I know you guys did something special."

"Yeah, us, maybe we did at that," Travis said with a forced laugh, trying his best to just go along with Chad so he could get into the bathroom, piss his guts out and shower again to try to relieve the pain in his asshole. "But truthfully, we didn't, Chad. I would tell you if we did."

"Damn, you guys are unbelievable," Chad said. "Totally designer guys. I mean, look at you now, even wearing designer underpants. The only designer and fashionable stuff I own is what my aunt sends me; like I've told you, she works for a men's fashion magazine in New York. If she didn't send me stuff, I would never know what to wear."

Travis could not believe that under all that musculature and fashionable Marcello haircut that this stupendously handsome guy was such a geek.

"You know, I've told you, man, any time you feel like dressing up and hanging out with us, you're more than welcome," Travis said.

To his dismay, every time his asshole twitched in pain, his erection leaked beads of piss and pre-cum in his boxer briefs, making an evident stain on the front of them and outlining his wide, sexy slit.

And it had not been lost on Travis how Chad had oh so innocently just mentioned his designer boxer briefs, stealing a glance at them as they bulged with his erection trickling inside.

"Thanks O'Toole, but I'm really not a suit and tie and thin dress sock sort of guy, I'm more the casual, laid back personal trainer type, you know? That's why my aunt sends me the sort of stuff you see me wearing," Chad said. "But, you know that I always appreciate the invite to join you and the suit men."

"Sure, sure thing, man," Travis responded. The look of misery that suddenly came over Travis' angelically handsome face did not go unnoticed by his roommate.

"Say, you okay there, bud?" Chad asked. "You uh, feel okay and all?"

"Uh, yeah, and no, Chad, I uh, sort of had a bad time of it after the game yesterday," Travis said. Without realizing what he was doing because of the pain he was in, he reached behind himself, stuck a hand down the back of his boxer briefs and massaged his aching hole with two fingers.

"Say, man, what's going on there?" Chad asked, curiously watching Travis standing there massaging his hole.

"Uh, like I said, man, I had a bad time of it after the game yesterday," Travis muttered as he massaged and prodded his own asshole, which caused his erection to harden beyond bulging in his designer boxer briefs.

"What happened, man?" Chad asked, sounding totally dumb and lame. "Maybe I can help you a bit, huh?"

"Uh, let us, let's just say that I've gotten myself into a pretty tight predicament and there's not much I can do about it until a good buddy of mine helps me out of it," Travis said, not noticing that Chad had made his way behind him and was now watching in amazement as Travis tried to massage the pain out of his poor wounded asshole.

"I think I know what you mean there, bud," Chad said.

Travis was confused. "You do?"

"Here, I'm sure I can help you out a bit," Chad said, then dropped to the floor behind him.

Scant seconds later, Chad pulled down the back section of Travis' boxer briefs, tucked them under his delectable ass cheeks, and then gently extracted the jock's finger from his hole before going to work on his wounded rear. Travis' jaw dropped nearly to the floor as he stood with his hands crossed behind his head.

He had never figured his roommate for being gay, but then Chad was just that, his roommate. They really hadn't shared more than that since they had met, except for the fact that Chad seemed to be in awe of Travis and his Suit Men buddies.

Travis' lips formed an "O" and he let out a sound like "OOOOOO" as he stood there. He felt his roommate grip his ass cheeks and spread them apart. The next thing Travis felt was Chad's tongue slithering deeply and sensuously into his opened back doorway.

Travis moaned loudly and swiveled sexily and involuntarily on his naked feet.

Chad's tongue seemed like it was working magic in the jock's most private crevice as he forced Travis' ass cheeks open wider still and spit in his hole a few times. If Travis had been wearing a pair of his silk dress socks, he was sure he would have jumped right out of them at that moment. Thank God for garters, he chuckled to himself. As Chad's saliva dripped against his ass walls, Travis felt his roommate planting delicate and sensual kisses in there as well.

"Who's been beating on your shit chute, O'Toole?" Chad asked, and then spit a few more times into Travis' hole, the saliva warm and comforting. "It looks all bruised and scratched back here."

"I—uh, I'd rather not say, bud," Travis replied as his cock pounded hard and like a thing alive in his boxer briefs.

His balls were churning like crazy as Chad again planted delicate feel-good kisses on his ass walls. The need to shoot a load and piss like a racehorse was overpowering. "It's a really complicated situation."

"Well, hopefully this will make it feel better, bud," Chad said, then spread Travis' delectable ass cheeks all the more, forcing his back door open and putting the jock's pink bunghole on display.

Travis bent over a bit and swooned as he then felt Chad's tongue lapping wonderfully at his wounded ass walls. It was soothing and maddening at the same time. Then Chad buried his face in between Travis' mounds and sucked at his walls like a bitch in heat.

Travis moaned louder as he bent over and gripped his naked, muscular, well-formed calves as his roommate performed the best remedy for his oh so wounded asshole.

"Feeling better, bud?" Chad asked as he slowly slid his face out from between Travis' ass walls.

"Ooooo yeah, *yeah,* you know it, man," Travis grunted as his erection oozed mounds of pre-seed, staining the front of his undershorts. "Oh God, Chad! Oh fuck, man."

Chad grinned from ear to ear and then puckered his lips and planted more delicate kisses on Travis' exposed bunghole, spitting in it a few times more as well for good measure.

"Okay, bud, now I need you to hold your cheeks wide open for me," Chad said a few moments later.

Without hesitating, Travis stood up straight and reached behind himself.

Holding his ass mounds in his football player size hands and gripping them tight, Travis spread them as wide as possible. Chad slathered a cold and chilling cream against the jock's wounded ass walls, his fingers working magic back there that Travis had *never* known, forcing Travis to dance involuntarily on his toes. Travis felt as if he could cum right there in his boxer briefs without his cock even being touched, but he controlled himself as best he could, for the jock had other plans for his steely piss filled erection.

"This cream should help your hole feel better, bud," Chad said as Travis' head spun and his cock churned and throbbed in his boxer briefs.

"Oooooo man, Chad, you can do this to me anytime, bud," Travis groaned as he held his ass cheeks tighter and pulled them as far apart as possible.

"Well, let's hope I won't have to, man. Whatever it is that happened to your hole shouldn't happen again," Chad said and then extracted his fingers from Travis' chute.

His roommate's fingers came out of Travis' asshole with a popping sound. Between having his hole spit in, licked, and his ass walls kissed along with the cream that Chad had slathered in there, Travis felt like a new man in the department of his back door. His roommate had really worked wonders for him, but now it was his roommate's turn to experience some backdoor action, Travis mused, suddenly feeling very dominant and in total control.

Abruptly, Travis whirled around, faced his roommate head-on and gripped Chad Towers' shoulders' tightly.

"What's up, bud?" Chad asked with a snide grin.

"I'm about to show you what's up, bud," Travis sneered, then whirled Chad around, facing away from him.

Chad grunted and then felt Travis' hands working at getting his jeans and underpants pulled down from behind.

In what seemed like seconds, Chad's jeans and underpants were pooled down around his booted ankles, his thick black socks peeking out of the top as Travis forcefully bent him over. This time it was Chad who was gripping his calves as Travis worked on his asshole with a vengeance.

With his big hands shaking and quaking, Travis spread Chad's ass cheeks far apart, spit into them a few times to sop and lube him up till he was wet as a fish's back in there and then stood up behind him, his cock raging hard in his designer boxer briefs.

"Oh fuck, yeah, Chad, you got me all worked up and hornier than a bitch in heat on a Saturday night," Travis railed.

With one hand, he shucked his boxer briefs down and stepped out of them while he spanked and kneaded Chad's exquisite ass mounds with the other.

"Gonna jam my fucking hard piss filled cock up your ass, bud. Oh fuck, yeah, gonna plow my cock right up your ass."

Travis, amazed that he sounded exactly like his skin, went to work, slowly inching his erection into his roommate's open back door.

Chad didn't resist Travis at all. If anything, this was what the guy had wanted since he and Travis had become roommates. Somehow he had known it would be just a matter of time, and he had played his cards right.

As Travis entered him, Chad let out a grunt of thanks with total animal-like satisfaction. For once, since having become Spike's bitch (for lack of a better word), Travis was the one in control.

"Fuck yeah, nice tight ass walls, Towers!" Travis said as he seethed and buried himself inside his roommate, slapping and clenching his sweet ass cheeks at the same time. "Oh fuck, man, I am goin' to shoot my load so far up your ass that you'll taste it, Towers!!"

Chad bent over further to accommodate Travis' huge nine-inch shaft. Chad had seen Travis in the nude plenty of times since they had become roommates; seen him after he had showered, while his cock was flaccid and dangling sexy between his muscular legs. Chad, like most other guys at Calderfield College, considered himself to be a straight dude, a macho dude, but somehow, like other guys there as well, there was just something about Travis O'Toole the Fourth that really rocked his world. And now the guy *was* rocking his world!

"Yeah, feel my cock up your ass, Towers. How's that feel, huh, bud?" Travis ranted and seethed and spanked Chad's ass cheeks till they were flaming red.

He thrust and shoved and propelled himself deeper into his roommate's rear.

"Feels awesome, O'Toole. Feels like you're splitting me in half back there," Chad said.

Then Travis reached forward, grabbed a handful of Chad's neatly styled Marcello haircut and yanked the guy straight up to his feet.

Chad grunted as Travis wrapped his big arms around him and pressed himself as close to him as possible, burying himself in Chad's anal opening.

"Oh fuck, man! I can plow you all day, Towers, all fucking day; my cock up your ass, my goddamned cock up your ass," Travis bellowed into his roommate's ear, planting kisses on the back of his neck as he went on and on fucking him. "I should take doses of Viagra and fuck you all day, all afternoon, all night, God!!!"

As Chad listened to Travis' evil, sexy rant, his own cock was hard as a flagpole and dripping pre-cum; his balls ached to unload the two days' worth of college boy seed that he had been harvesting in them.

"Oh, fuck, O'Toole, you're gonna get my nut juice for sure, bud," Chad exclaimed as he gripped his cock and began stroking it with a vengeance.

The sound of the two college boys in searing heat filled the dorm room as they shot their potent and powerful loads, Travis into Chad's well-fucked anal canal and Chad all over his own chest, nipples, stomach and pecs.

"Aw, fuck, Towers, holy fuck, *fucking fuck,* nice tight hole you got here, roomie. I love the way it's hugging my damned nine inches of fuck meat!" Travis seethed in his roommate's ear.

As Travis held Chad tight against him, Chad eventually let go of his spurting cock and gripped his roommate's muscular and powerful forearms.

"Oh God, O'Toole, I've wanted and prayed for this since we were paired up as roommates," Chad panted as he felt Travis' cock shriveling inside him. "I mean, fuck, I'm straight as they come, got a girlfriend and all that, bud, but there is something heavy duty about that cock of yours, man."

"Yeah, glad to hear that, bud. Sometimes prayers are answered after all, huh?" Travis crooned, still maintaining his powerfully driven aura.

As Travis' cock softened inside his roommate, it slowly slid from Chad's asshole.

"Fuck, I wish I had some Viagra right now," Travis muttered. "I would plow you all over again, that ass of yours is worth it, Towers."

"Your wish is my command," Chad said with a grin, reaching down to his pants pooled around his ankles, then into one of the pockets and bringing out a little blue pill.

Travis grinned and popped the pill into his mouth.

A few moments later, the two roommates were in the shower and Travis was again fucking Chad Towers' delectable asshole, seeming not to be able to get enough of it.

6

While Travis O'Toole the fourth was having a sexual romp in his college dorm room with his roommate, John Broderick was speaking to his dad on the phone.

"I'm telling you, Dad, O'Toole's son is paying for what his dad did to you in ways that you cannot believe," John said. "When that boss of yours finds out what I got on his pretty-boy son and what I've turned him into, he'll admit that he set you up; and if he doesn't, well, I got a video here that—"

John's words were cut off when he heard the insistent knocking on the door.

"Shit, there he is now," John said. "I have a date at a tuxedo shop with the dude today, Dad. I'm making him not only outfit me in a tuxedo by Armani and maybe one by Versace, but pay for it as well."

John listened as his dad again proclaimed his innocence and told him how much he appreciated what his son was doing for him.

"Not to worry, Dad," John said. "You'll be cleared and out of prison before you know it."

Then the loud banging at the door sounded again.

"Okay, O'Toole, I'm coming!" John shouted, then told his dad good-bye and hung up the phone.

Dressed in a white button down shirt by Geoffrey Beane, black skinny jeans by Calvin Klein and lace-up ankle length black dress boots by Cole Haan, all purchased for him by Travis, John made his way to the door, a shit eating grin etched on his face.

"You got here early, O'Toole," John said as he sauntered to the door. "I suppose you want to get to the tuxedo shop and get this over with, huh?" John called out. "But I have other uses in mind for you before we head to the shop, buddy, because I'm feeling all horny and worked up again."

John opened the door to find not Travis, but Spike.

"Hello asshole," Spike said, and then blew a mouthful of cigarette smoke into John's face.

"Wh—what the, who the fuck are you?" John asked, then realized. "*Shit,* you're the trucker who worked over that jock pussy!"

"He's *my* jock pussy!" Spike railed, and then delivered a swooping fist down hard on John's face.

John howled in pain as he stumbled back into his dorm room, landing on the floor on his back as Spike stepped in and closed and locked the door behind him.

"Fucking shit head, fucking shit for brains, lookit you all dressed up like my boy," Spike said as he stepped next to John's prone body and kicked him hard in the ribs with his booted foot.

"WWHHHUUUUFFF," was the sound that escaped John then. "Fuck, man, you get the hell outa here now or I'll—"

"You'll what???" Spike thundered down at the guy. "You'll do shit, bud! Actually, you're gonna do everything *I* tell you. You see, I ain't the jock pussy."

Again, Spike's booted foot connected with John's ribs.

John howled again in pain, and then tried to crawl toward the phone.

"I'll have the cops here to make short work of you, lowlife," John sniveled.

Spike let loose with an evil laugh. The skinhead reached down and grabbed John by a handful of his hair.

John screamed in pain as Spike literally hoisted him upward by his hair. John pressed his palms against the floor and tried to pull himself to a kneeling position.

But as he did so, Spike pressed a booted foot against John's rear and kicked him back to the floor.

"Where's the video?" Spike asked. "And I want *all* the copies you made, asshole. And God help you if you gave any copies to any of your asshole buddies, if someone like you even *has* a buddy, that is."

John quickly turned onto his back and looked up at Spike.

"I'll never give you the goddamned video," John railed.

Spike reached down, grabbed the guy by his booted ankles and hoisted him to an upside down position, swinging him as he went.

"Yahhhhh!!! You fucking scum, put me down!!" John demanded.

"Sure thing, asshole," Spike said, then spit down into John's face and let go of his ankles, sending the guy headfirst to the floor.

John railed in pain again as his head hit the floor hard.

"Where's the video?" Spike asked again. As John looked up at him, Spike pressed his booted foot over the guy's neck. "Where is the fucking video, asshole?"

John gasped, then said, "Fuck man, if, if you kill me, you'll never get it."

Spike pressed his foot harder against John's windpipe.

"I can work you over all day, asshole, *where's the video?*" Spike asked again.

"Bastard, that jock pussy will be here soon, and him and me got a shopping date for him to buy me a tuxedo," John roared up at Spike, who then pressed his foot harder against John's throat.

"That shopping date has just been canceled, asshole," Spike said, then took his foot off John's throat, reached down and grabbed the guy by the front section of his hair and pulled.

"YAHHHHHH!!!" John roared as Spike hauled him up and forward and then literally flung him across the room, causing John to land on his stomach.

As John lay in a heap, gasping, he felt the Cole Haan dress boots being yanked right off his feet.

"All the stuff that my boy bought you is goin' back, asshole! You ain't worthy enough to be dressin' like he does," Spike growled.

Then, at the sight of the silk black socks that John had on, Spike seethed, clenched his teeth and kicked John across his left ankle.

"Fuck, what are you doin' wearin' silk socks??? You ain't a suit guy; you ain't no jock, *fucker!!* You can take this to the bank for sure; my boy won't be buyin' you anymore clothes or men's jewelry, for that matter!"

"Owwww!!! My ankle, you moron!!" John shrilled.

"It's gonna be a lot more than your ankle very soon, *moron!!*" Spike railed at the college student. "I ain't got no problem, *no problem* whatsoever in breaking every bone in your goddamned body. Believe me, it would be a pleasure to hear those bones of yours snapping! Now, *where's the video???*"

Spike raised his foot to kick John's naked ankle again when John screamed up at him, "Do you know what your jock pussy's dad did to my dad???"

In response, Spike kicked John's ankle a second time, harder.

"Owwwwww Gawd!!!" John cried.

"I'm sure I don't give a rat's ass what my boy's dad did to your dad," Spike said. "What I care about is him *and* the video. Where is it, asshole???"

"Fucker, go to hell!!!" John responded, this time spitting up at Spike.

The skinhead clenched his teeth, curled one of his big hands into a fist and pummeled it hard across John's jaw.

John moaned as two of his teeth came flying out of his mouth, followed by a trail of blood that flowed liberally over his lips.

A few moments later, Spike had John in the bathroom, sat him down on the closed toilet lid, and held up John's electric shaver. John was now shirtless, as Spike had gotten his white button down off him as soon as he had seen the blood from the guy's mouth trailing toward it. The skinhead wanted his jock pussy boy to be able to return all the merchandise that he had been blackmailed into buying for John in good shape, plus, there would be no need for him to be wearing any sort of shirt, or pants where Spike intended to take him.

Blood from John's trembling mouth landed on his naked chest as Spike shaved off his eyebrows.

"What the fuck are you doing to me, man???" John howled as the pain in his mouth intensified and his chest became even redder with blood.

The college student could not believe that any passerby in the hallway did not respond to his screams of agony. Given his reputation as a user and a troublemaker, it wasn't hard to understand why any screams from John Broderick would be ignored.

Spike spat into John's face, then said, "Where's the video? I'll shave your head next and then your chest, and then your cock area. See if I won't, asshole!!"

"Fuck you!!!" John screamed and blood landed on Spike's leather vest.

Spike again clenched his teeth and trailed the shaver harder over John's eyebrows.

John did not for a second raise his hands to Spike, seeing as the guy was holding the clippers.

Then Spike yanked John up off the toilet lid by his hair and stood him in front of the mirror over the sink.

"Look how pretty you're not now, asshole, with a bloody mouth and no eyebrows!!" Spike said, then slammed John's forehead against the mirror, breaking the glass and gashing his forehead.

John screamed, then pressed his right hand against his now blood-ied forehead and reached down and turned on the cold water with his left.

As Spike stood there snickering, the electric shaver still buzzing in his hand, he watched as the pathetic and terror-stricken John Broderick sluiced water into his bloody mouth and over his forehead, trying to staunch the flow of blood.

"You bastard, look what you've—"

Spike raised a booted foot and slammed it against the backs of John's calves.

John lost his balance and slid to the floor as his chin slammed against the top of the sink, loosening two more of his front teeth and causing more blood to spill from his mouth.

"Gawd, man," John cried pitifully now.

As John lay on the bathroom floor whimpering and sniveling mis-erably in pain, Spike reached down, and with a few pulls, yanked the guy's designer jeans off him, leaving John clad in just his silk socks and a pair of white silk underpants, all bought for him by Travis.

"These are also goin' back to the store, asshole," Spike said.

"Y—you son of a bitch," John gurgled as blood splattered from his mouth all over the bathroom floor.

Then Spike went to work shearing John's head.

"Where's the video?" Spike asked again.

As John's wavy locks hit the floor and mixed with his blood, Spike said, "I don't have an off switch, asshole, I can work you over all fucking day. I'm gonna be in your face until you produce that video and all the copies of it, too!'

"Fucking bastard!!!" John screamed as he was forced to look at his bald and eyebrow-less face in the broken mirror above the sink. "What have you done to me, man??? What have you done???"

"This is just the beginning, asshole," Spike said, then grabbed John by the back of his silk underpants and turned him around, facing him.

"Hey, what the fuck," John began when he saw the electric shaver now headed for his chest.

He squeezed his eyes shut and gripped the sink behind him.

John's shriveled cock spurted beads of piss into his silk underpants as Spike meanly and cruelly sheared from his stomach region all the way up to just below the college student's neckline.

As he felt his chest hair being shaved off, John stood there shaking and quaking in his silk socks, trying not to piss in his briefs.

Next, John still did not raise a hand to Spike as the guy then lowered his silk briefs in front of him, tucked them under his testicles and went to work shaving off his pubic bush, holding the tip of what he called John's pathetic penis in his fingertips.

"Oh, please man, be careful down there," John begged as his pubic bush was sheared away.

"You think I give a rat's ass if I accidentally slice off this cock of yours, you asshole?" Spike replied and squeezed the tip of John's cock harder. "You fucked my boy with this cock. *You fucked my boy!!*"

John whimpered and said silent prayers as Spike finished shaving away his pubic bush and then went to work shaving the hair off his sac.

"Fucking asshole, who said you had dibs on my jock pussy? What kind of guy does to another dude what you did to my boy?" Spike seethed.

When he was done shaving John's sac, Spike let go of the guy, rapped him hard across the face again and sent John sprawling once more to the floor.

"Let's go, asshole," Spike said as he reached down, grabbed one of John's silk socked ankles and dragged him from the bathroom back to the center of the dorm room.

John cried in misery and pain as Spike looked around the room until he spotted exactly what he needed.

"Ah, that'll work just fine, and how great that you have a giant sized one at that," Spike said.

A short while later, Spike was walking out of John's dorm room lugging a huge laundry bag over his shoulder. The skinhead thanked whatever gods were watching over him that there was nobody in the hallway to witness him. But just to be on the safe side, in case anyone was looking out of peepholes from the other dorm rooms, he yelled behind him, "Take care, John. It was really good to see you, man. I'll have all this laundry of yours done for you soon."

When Travis arrived at John's dorm room about ten minutes after Spike had left, he was surprised to find that John was not there. The handsome jock boy wondered if his blackmailer had forgotten about their appointment at the tuxedo shop.

7

Bart Findley screamed in pain as his asshole was rammed by Jerome for what felt like the umpteenth time.

"You lowlife bastards, this is a shitty thing to be doing to a football player of my caliber!!" Bart cried out. "Uhhhhhhh!!!"

"Oh man, feels so sweet and tight in there, Mr. Football de-lite," Jerome exclaimed as he held Bart's powerful legs up in the air by the college football player's navy blue sheer socked calves and spread them wide.

Jerome speared him and speared him, thrusting in and out of the muscle bound guy's exposed and gaping hole.

As Jerome repeatedly rammed him, Bart felt the black skinhead's kiwi-sized nuts banging against his ass. This was the second time during the second day of his captivity that Bart had been used this way by Jerome. And to add insult to injury, even though he was blindfolded, the football god knew that the other black skinheads from the day before were in the room as well.

"Aw shit, I—I can't believe this is gonna happen again," Bart said, his roped hands behind his back curled into big fists.

His big testicles churned as Jerome's cock head rubbed against his sphincter.

"Oh holy fuck, you bastards!!" Bart railed. To his disbelief, and without his fear-hard cock even being touched or squeezed or yanked, he shot his load all over his massively muscular chest, pecs, stomach regions and nipples.

Bart seethed and screamed as the pain in his hole caused by Jerome's gargantuan cock stretching his asshole suddenly intensified to what felt like a thousand percent more.

"Please, s—stop, please stop! Oh gawd, you guys, I shot my load again," Bart moaned.

"Sho nuff did shoot that load again, best bud of the jock pussy," Jerome grunted as he relentlessly and persistently jammed his steely erection deeper and deeper inside the football captive. "Seems like whenever yo butt-hole is fucked real well yo shoot your load, fucking white boys just loves bein' fucked by black men's big meat sticks."

"No, no, that's not true, you bast—" Bart began, but was cut off by Jerome's iron-like grip squeezing his socked calves. Jerome took a guttural breath and let loose with his second load of ball juice into Bart's rectum.

"Oh, fuck, man, yo ain't as sweet as the jock pussy is, but yo rear door sho nuff is dee-fucking-lectable," Jerome said through his clenched pearly white teeth as he drained his cock into Bart's rear.

As Jerome splooged torrents of cum inside of him, Bart's cock dribbled out the last of his latest cum shot as well.

"Plea— please, no more. Please let me go," Bart begged as Jerome lowered the football player's massive legs to the massage table that he was stretched out on.

Once again, eight mouths converged on the football god's chest, stomach, pecs and nipples and ate and sucked his latest cum offering off him.

Bart screamed, arching his blindfolded head back a bit and feeling totally beyond sensitized as he was again devoured.

"Mmm, white boy milkshake," Darren, Jerome's best buddy, said in between sucking the cum off one of Bart's very chewed up and worked over nipples.

The eight black skinheads, stripped to just sneakers and sweat socks–Jerome, Darren, Malik, Willie, Reginald, Jamal and Maurice–were all gathered around the football stud in the sauna they had brought him to the night before. As Bart Findley lay there with his hands bound tightly behind him and blindfolded with a stinking white discarded sweat sock, he gasped and grunted and sweated as the eight skinheads all licked and sucked his cum off his massive torso.

"You bastards, when in all fucks are you guys gonna let me go???" Bart railed miserably. To his dismay, he felt his socked calves gripped again and his legs being spread wide and hoisted into the air. "Oh no, no, oh please, not again!! Oh God, oh my poor asshole, you guys!!!"

Then Bart felt another huge black cock spear him slowly, inch by painful inch, as this time it was Darren taking his second turn at the football player's rear end.

"Do that answer your question, Mr. Football player in his pretty sheer socks?" Darren asked, chuckling down at Bart, at the same time glorying in the fact that this handsome god-like white guy was their sex slave.

Livid and feeling beyond disbelief over the events that had played out over the last twenty-four hours or so, Bart fumed.

"What a twisted turn of events this has all been," Bart reeled.

"Spoken like a true college boy," Darren said and all eight of the skinheads laughed meanly, all of them hard as steel and anxiously awaiting their turns at Bart's rear.

"I swear to you mugs, my football buds will get you guys for this!" Bart threatened.

"Ah, but will they get you?" Darren asked as he slid his hard cock deeper inside the football player. "Because we don't plan on givin' you back to your football buds any time soon, Mr. Football de-lite."

"Uh, no, you can't mean that," Bart begged, then felt Darren's cock tip kissing his sphincter. "Oh, fuck, and here it goes again!"

As the skinhead's cock tip teased Bart's sphincter and innards, Bart felt his own cock *again* rising to the occasion. The football god knew that the only other time in his life that his rear had been toyed with and he had perked and shot his load without his cock even being touched was when a girl he had been dating and her sorority roommate had had the audacity to trick him into bondage, tying him to one of the twin beds in their room and then using an assortment of dildos on his exposed rear end. It was humiliating, yet he had learned a few things about himself. Had he not experienced being fucked with a dildo, he would not understand why he was shooting his load every time the skinheads plowed his poor asshole. But the time that the girl he had been dating and her roommate had had their fun with his asshole, he was a willing participant. This time he was *not* willing, this time he had been literally kidnapped and carried off into sexual captivity.

As Darren fucked him furiously and hard, Bart recalled the girl he had been dating nearly six months ago. Her name was Lisa, she was blond, just shy of five feet seven inches tall, had blue eyes that pierced the football player to his very soul and a set of the biggest tits he had ever seen, or had the pleasure of feasting on for hours on end, before she had managed to convince him to let her tie him to her headboard.

Bart and Lisa had met in a physics class at Calderfield College, a course that both of the students were required to take. From the moment Lisa saw the tall, dark haired suited Bart Findley, she admitted that he truly got her juices flowing.

She hadn't spoken to him the first few times she saw him in class, but she had told her bi-sexual roommate, Karen, about him. The kinky Karen knew that he would be good fodder for the games she and Lisa enjoyed playing. So, during a night of hot, passionate lesbian sex, Karen formulated a plan so that Lisa and she could have some sinister and sexy fun with the handsome football player, Bart Findley. Karen assured Lisa that in the end, he would come (and cum and cum and cum) away wanting more of what she intended to put him through.

"Football players love having their endurance levels tested," Karen whispered in Lisa's ear that night as the two young sorority sisters lay side by side in Karen's bed.

Karen squeezed and twisted one of Lisa's very erect and nubile nipples as she whispered her plan.

Lisa's pussy juice flowed like a river and all she could do was say yes, yes she would serve up Bart Findley as a sexual sacrifice to her roommate. The two young women wanted him enough and he was handsome and muscular enough to fit the desires they felt, twisted as those desires were. After seeing Bart on the Calderfield College football field in all his football and macho glory, and then with his buddies, The Suit Men, the two young sorority sisters had decided that Bart Findley's sexual fate with them was sealed.

Fate was on Lisa's side the day their physics professor teamed her up with Bart for a class project. It was during that project that Lisa made comments on how she loved the fact that Bart came to class dressed in his designer suits, complete with all the accessories, down to his well-shined lace-up shoes and even the sheer socks he chose rather than just ordinary solid-colored dress socks. Bart was instantly flattered, and while they worked on their physics project, he told Lisa of his buddies, The Suit Men. She said she had seen them on campus and then she pretended to realize who Bart was, seeing as he and his best buddy, Travis O'Toole, were the star players on the Calderfield College football team.

Bart was even more flattered at that point. So flattered that he asked Lisa what she was doing that coming Saturday night. She blushed and said, "I thought you would never ask, Mr. Findley," and instantly accepted his invitation to dinner at a highbrow restaurant near the college campus. When she kissed his lips oh so gently and suggested that after dinner at the restaurant they would have a special dessert in her dorm room, Bart's cock went from flaccid to hard in his suit pants in mere seconds. He grinned sexily at her and agreed to her proposal as well.

For Bart Findley, that Saturday evening could not come fast enough, not to mention that he would not cum fast enough either. He had asked Lisa out on Tuesday afternoon and vowed to save himself from shooting his load till that Saturday evening on their date, somehow knowing that she intended to really rock his world. During the rest of the week, Bart found it beyond difficult to concentrate on his classes. When he was out at the snack bar with The Suit Men, he bragged about his upcoming date with the beautiful and sexy Lisa from his physics class.

* * *

"Yeah, fuckin' cumming inside Mr. Football de-lite!!" Darren crowed loudly, bringing Bart back to the here-and-now. "Oh fuck yeah, feels great, Football de-lite, your hole sucking in my sperm offering!!"

"You bastard!!!" was the blindfolded and tied up football player's pain-filled response.

Bart felt Darren's warm ball juice flooding his anal opening as the guy relentlessly thrust in and out of him, his shaft gliding against the football player's ass walls and teasing his sphincter deep down inside. But then, to Bart's utter disbelief, he astounded himself yet again as he shot his own load once more, in small spurts this time, all over his torso. He and Darren roared and grunted like two captured marines as they each shot their loads, Darren in outright pleasure and Bart in confusion, pain and with his head spinning in what seemed like a reverse sort of orbit.

"Cumming again, fucking cumming again," Bart cried as he shot his load, his balls aching as they put forth his sperm in spurts.

"Fuck me man, that shit is un-fucking believable," Darren said with a laugh as his cock softened and slid slowly out of the football player's rectum. "Every time he's fucked, he cums."

All the men in the room laughed. After Bart's legs were set down, the men once more swarmed downward and ate the football player's good stuff off his torso, sucking and slurping at him like vampires. Bart sweated and screeched as his hyper-sensitive muscular body was feasted on once more.

"I really am their goddamned meat market," Bart thought as he cried miserably behind his blindfold.

When Bart felt his legs being lifted yet again, he clenched his teeth and reeled in pain as this time it was Darnell, one of the black skinheads who loved torturing his balls, fucking the football player's asshole.

Bart bellowed and felt like he would lose his mind when he felt the enormity of Darnell's cock as it squeezed its way into him.

"Oh, you fucker, whoever you are," Bart sniveled.

"Now you know why we blindfolded those pretty peepers of yo's, no way yo will know who be fucking you Football de-lite," Darnell exclaimed as Bart's ass walls sucked his enormous cock deep inside.

As Darnell entered Bart, he pushed the football player's legs up, up and up until the bottoms of Bart's socked feet were looking at the ceiling.

Bart screamed as Darnell plunged deeper into him, feeling like he was ripping the golden boy in two. Bart felt his balls churning and cooking up more sperm, and his mind drifted back again to the first time his asshole had been used in such a degrading, yet erotic, manner.

On the Saturday night of his date with Lisa, Bart had dressed to the nines in a brown suit by Versace, white shirt by Hermes and a beige silk power tie, also by Hermes. For his footwear, Bart chose lace-up chocolate colored, well-shined cap-toes by Florsheim, a favorite store of his dad's, and sheer thick and thin OTC brown ribbed socks by Stacy Adams, part of a three pack gift that his best buddy, Travis, had given him. Anything that Travis gave Bart, Bart considered a good luck charm. But on this night, he had to wonder just which way his luck had actually run.

After a most romantic dinner by candlelight at a highbrow restaurant called The Three Forks, a most fitting name for the way the evening would wind out, while he and Lisa ate a steak dinner each, the football player had no clue what the number three would mean.

After dinner, Bart escorted Lisa back to her dorm room, the two of them holding hands as they walked slowly through the college campus.

"I must say, that was a wonderful dinner," Lisa said. She wore a very tight fitting black, thigh length dress by Anne Taylor, black stockings and high-heeled black leather pumps by Jimmy Choo.

"I'm glad you enjoyed it," Bart said, squeezing Lisa's hand tighter as they walked. He loved how her dress showed off just enough of her cleavage to tease him.

But teasing time would soon be over, or so Bart thought.

"I just can't believe you didn't want to try their flaming arrow for dessert. It's a round tart with a light solid chocolate in the center," Bart said.

Lisa stopped walking and looked up at him adoringly. "You're all the dessert I'm going to want, Mr. Football Findley," Lisa said almost breathlessly. "What I have planned for dessert will be something you will never forget, and trust me on this, Mr. Findley, your arrow will soon be flaming."

"Whoooo-wheeee," Bart said with a chuckle, then smiled a smile that could tear the ladies' hearts out.

He and Lisa walked on toward her dorm room at a slightly faster pace.

As Darnell shot his load into Bart, once more flooding the captive football player's rectum with black skinhead ball juice, Bart's thoughts were forced back to the present and his dire predicament.

It was now twenty-four hours since Bart Findley had been captured by Jerome and Darren. The poor football player still could not believe how easily and craftily he had been snagged right out of the college locker room. It was unthinkable, yet in the world of rivalry football, not so unheard of. But never had the football player heard of a dude being captured for such heinous reasons as what he was enduring. After having been feasted on, the unwitting and chewed up football player then found himself being introduced to the art of cock sucking, courtesy of his eight black skinhead captors. And then, to add true insult to injury, after having been forced to suck all their cocks and swallow all their loads numerous times, the eight black skinheads had then used Bart's mouth as a urinal, turning the captured football player into a human toilet, so to speak.

Twenty-four hours later, Bart Findley's mouth and throat still tasted of cum and piss as he found himself stretched out like a side of beef in the sleazy gym's steam room, atop a massage table.

The steam room turned out to be, for Bart Findley, the next room that he would come (and cum) to see (or not to see, seeing as the skinheads decided to blindfold the football player for his next sexual degradations) as a torture chamber in this gym of horrors, as he had come to call it; a gym like no other he had ever known in all his twenty-one years.

When he had been taken off the bench, Bart Findley struggled like a madman as he was held tight by various pairs of huge hands. Bart's hands were bound tightly behind him and his socked feet were tied tightly together as well. He then found himself blindfolded and being lugged by Jerome and Darren down yet another flight of stairs, deeper, it seemed, into the entrails of the gym, which now felt more like a prison yard than a gym.

As he lay there feeling like a side of raw beef and being feasted on like some cheap whore, Bart's mind was awhirl with memories of his kinky girlfriend Lisa and also of how he had been taken from the locker room where Jerome and Darren had tied him to a bench to be used and debased. Bart was amazed and confused by how the two events, so opposite, yet so similar, seemed to affect him.

This was all too much to be believed.

"Okay, okay, I'm oh so fucking glad that all of you are feeling real good and even first-rate here, and I'm really glad to be made to shoot my load like this, humiliating as it is for me, dudes," Bart thundered angrily from where he lay like a sacrificial lamb on an altar. "But I would appreciate it at this point if you guys would PLEASE let me the fuck out of here! You've all had your twisted fun with me and… oh Gawd!!!"

But then, Bart's words were cut short as Darren plowed into him for the second time.

"Let you go, Mr. Football de-lite?" Darren asked Bart as he hoisted his legs high and plowed deep, deep, deep inside him. "Man, some of that there piss that we fed you must have been spiked, 'cause we ain't gonna be lettin' you go fo' some time."

As he was fucked deeper and deeper, Bart's eyes opened wide in terror under his sock blindfold and he could only scream out more and more in pain as he was fucked hard.

But Bart Findley had to be brutally honest with himself. He had known that once the door to the sauna had locked behind the skins, that he would not be leaving the sleazy gym that day. He hoped and prayed that his buddies from his classes would wonder where the fuck he was, that he hadn't been seen since the victorious football game, and that they would come looking for him. If it was one thing that Bart's buddies knew about him, as much as he cherished being a football player, he cherished his good grades as well. He was *never* late or absent from classes unless it was totally unavoidable. But even on that score, Bart did not hold out much hope, seeing as no one, *no one* knew he had been so cleverly captured and spirited off from the college locker room. If any of his football buds, or even The Suit Men, heard about his capture, they would more than likely see it as the antics of the football team they had bested that day, and no real harm would come to him, *right!*

"You bastards, you *fucking* sick bastards, like I've told you guys over and over, WHAT A TWISTED AND FUCKED UP TURN OF EVENTS this has been for a football player of my caliber," Bart swore as he tugged and struggled like a madman on the ropes binding him. "Fucking dudes, what kind of men are you??? First you fucking devour me like I'm a side of beef, then you make me eat your cum and drink your piss!!! I swear, my stomach feels like it's gonna hurl!!!"

"Nah, you be okay, white boy," Jamal, one of the foot fetish skinheads said, then leaned down and kissed the tip of one of Bart's big toes under his sheer blue OTC sock.

At the beginning of his capture, while his asshole was still virginal, (Har, har, har) Bart thought back to a day while he was out at the food court with his buddies, The Suit Men, and he was told of a college football rivalry that had supposedly surpassed all others in the history of college football rivalries. It was Suit Man Steve who had told the story of a football player who had been very cleverly abducted and left tied up and blindfolded to a bed in a female sorority house on a college campus.

After the football player's blindfold had been removed, he was forced to lie on the bed in total bondage while his his cock and mouth were used to service some of the evil girlfriends of the rival football team. When the bitches had finally released the football player, he was one very exhausted but happy dude. Of course, this was just an urban legend, as there was nothing substantial to back it up, and no college football player had ever come forward to admit that it had happened to him. But Bart had to admit that when he had heard about it, he was furiously jealous of whoever the supposedly kidnapped football player was. The thought of being used and sexually abused by a group of horned up sexy bitches was just too much for the young, handsome jock to contemplate without getting a hard-on the size of a flagpole. But to be used in the way that the eight black skinheads were presently using and abusing him, well, in the captured jock's opinion, this was not one for the history books, or even for urban legends.

On the night of his date with Lisa, when they arrived back at her college dorm room, Lisa had Bart stripped to his beige silk, tight fitting briefs by 21XST and his OTC brown thick and thin ribbed sheer socks by Stacy Adams faster than the jock could run on the football field. When they had entered her dorm room and she flipped on the lights, Bart did not say a word at the sight of the leather wrist restraints hanging from the sides of the headboard. Instead, he was instantly hard and boned, his cock tenting his beige briefs and suit pants.

"Oh my God," Bart whispered as he stood next to the bed.

He leaned down and kissed Lisa on the lips over and over as she slowly slid out of her dress, letting him see the sight of her sexy black bra by Victoria's Secret, under which her nipples pressed provocatively against the sexy cotton material.

As Bart leaned down to kiss Lisa's tits, she grabbed him by a handful of his hair and yanked his head up and away from her chest.

"Not yet," she whispered, then slowly slinked down on the side of her twin bed and into a seated position.

As Bart stood over her on his socked feet, Lisa reached forward and hooked her slender fingers around the sides of his briefs.

"Oh God, Lisa," Bart whispered, almost crying with joy as she slid his silk briefs off him and down to his ankles.

As the football player stepped out of his briefs and gently kicked them aside, he slid to his knees in front of Lisa, wrapped his huge, muscular arms around her and undid the clasp of her bra, nuzzling his lips against her neck while kissing and nibbling on her. The sounds of Lisa's moans of pleasure made Bart's hard cock engorge even more. His balls churned as they hung low between his tree-trunk like thighs as he leaned forward as Lisa wrapped a hand behind his bull-sized neck.

"Oh Lisa," Bart moaned passionately, and then began gently licking her very erect nipples, sucking on them hard and enduringly, sending chills through her very being.

As Bart's mouth worked its magic, Lisa rocked back and forth on the bed, her eyes darting and glancing at the bedroom closet.

As he licked and sucked her tits some more, Bart trailed the first two fingers of his right hand over her moist pussy, slowly inserting his fingers as well, having them come out drenched with her juices. Lisa watched and gasped as Bart stuck his fingers in his mouth and slurped them clean.

"Lisa, Lisa," he whispered as she coaxed him up onto the bed, leaned him against the headboard and began delicately kissing him everywhere.

Lisa pressed her lips against Bart's Adam's apple, kissed it and then kissed long and hard against the sides of his big neck, working her way down to his massive chest, pecs and nipples. When she pressed her lips against one of his nipples, Bart felt as if he could fly right out of his socks. She sucked his nipple a bit and pressed the palms of her hands against the sides of the football player's huge arms as he lay there with a steel hard erection.

"Oh God, oh Lisa," Bart moaned and squeezed his eyes shut as she then kissed and licked all over his stomach as he reached up and grabbed the sides of the headboard. "Feels awesome, so fucking awesome what you're doing to me, Lisa."

Lisa did not allow for the opportunity for escape, nor would she allow Bart to escape. As Lisa raised one of Bart's wrists toward the restraint hanging on the headboard, she pressed one of her tits against his handsome face. Once Lisa's tit was again in Bart's mouth and being sucked on, the football player was oblivious to everything that was going on around him.

Inside the closet, Karen's pussy became moist as she watched her roommate secure Bart's right wrist to the restraint hanging at the end of the headboard.

As Bart sucked Lisa's tit, he then felt his wrist being locked into the restraint.

"Ooo, you really are a kinky girl, huh, Lisa?" Bart asked, then glanced over and up at his secured wrist as Lisa took her tit from his mouth and quickly went to work securing his other wrist.

"You really don't know the half of it, Bart," Lisa whispered in his ear after both his wrists were securely locked into the leather restraints, stretching out his muscular arms while keeping his back against the headboard.

Lisa served Bart one of her tits, and as he chuckled and played along with her, sucking and nipping at her tit, he felt it. As Lisa caressed the back of his neck, Bart suddenly cried out, "Whaaaaa!" as he suddenly felt hands massaging one of his socked feet at the end of the bed.

"L—Lisa, what's, what the hell is going on??" Bart asked, looking up at Lisa as her breast hung in his face.

In response, Karen took hold of Lisa's breast, placed it back into Bart's mouth and commanded him to suck it.

The sounds of Bart sucking on Lisa's delectable nipple filled the room as the football player also felt his left foot being sensually massaged at the end of the bed. Bart's cock plumped up big and erect as the two women really began working him over.

8

After managing to easily overpower John Broderick and spiriting him out of his dorm room in an over-sized laundry bag, Spike was now driving his pickup truck along a deserted and lonely road, toward upstate New York. Behind the wheel, Spike drove calmly and with a shit-eating grin, a cigarette hanging out of the side of his mouth (as usual) and a sleazy punk-rock song blaring out of the speakers.

As he drove, Spike recalled how his jock pussy boy, his angel, had told him of the things that John was doing to him. It was unthinkable to Spike that someone could do to Travis what John was doing to him, heaping on him, abusing him constantly. Spike knew that it would not take long for his jock pussy, his angel, to lose his mind; and then his grades would plummet, and where would he be? If Spike allowed these goings-on to continue, poor Travis would never become the high-powered executive he dreamed of someday being.

Leering meanly through the windshield, Spike thought of the day that he had unexpectedly found Travis standing beside the garbage dumpster in the trash alley at The Cherry Hill Mall. Spike had been about to light a fresh cigarette as he was sauntering past the alley, toward the parking lot of the mall, when he saw the handsome and regally dressed Travis standing beside the dumpster.

"Well, well, and fucking well, to what do I owe this displeasure?" Spike joked meanly as he stepped into the alley, his big black work boots stomping loud against the pavement as he took in the sight of Travis standing there, clad in a light grey shark skin suit, a pink dress shirt, a pink and grey tightly knotted necktie, very low-cut slip-on grey shoes and sheer grey socks.

When Travis heard Spike's voice, he glanced up for all of a second, and when he saw his skin approaching, his cigarette still not lit, Travis instantly lowered his head, looked down at the ground and jammed his hands into the pockets of his pants.

"Hey there, jock pussy boy, no classes today at that fancy, shit-eating college of yours?" Spike asked, standing real close to Travis so that his cigarette smelling breath was wafting directly into Travis' nostrils. "Speak, and speak all you want while we're here today, jock pussy."

Travis slowly lifted his head and looked into Spike's deranged and dangerous looking eyes, not really wanting to peel his stare away from the big scuffed up work boots that the skin was wearing that day.

"N—no Sir, I actually do have classes today," Travis responded. When Spike saw the tears in Travis' eyes, he knew that this was not a time for stripping and debasing his boy in the trash alley.

Something was amiss here, and the skinhead meant to find out exactly what it was.

"But I can't go to those classes, because you see Sir, I'm uh, I'm having trouble sitting down these last few says, Sir," Travis went on and brought a gold cigarette lighter out of the right side pocket of his pants.

"Having trouble sitting down?" Spike asked as Travis flicked the lighter and held the flame with a shaking hand to Spike's cigarette tip.

Spike cupped his grubby, filthy hands around Travis' well-manicured one and felt how it was quaking as he puffed on his now lit cigarette, deliberately making the smoke waft into Travis' beautifully handsome face. The smell of Polo cologne by Ralph Lauren filled the air as Spike inhaled the scent of his special jock pussy boy. When Spike's cigarette was lit, Travis put the gold lighter back in his pants pocket.

"Got that lighter just for me, huh, jock pussy?" Spike asked and tweaked the knot in Travis' tie, squeezing it like it was a nipple.

"Sir, yes Sir," Travis replied.

"So, why in all fucks can't you sit down in your classes?" Spike asked. "You can't be missing classes, you know that."

"It, it's a horrible explanation, Sir. You see, the guy I told you about, the one who videotaped us the day you were going to tow my car," Travis sputtered, and without having to be told to do so, snapped to a stance of military attention as he spoke to his skinhead.

"Yeah, that loser named John," Spike replied and trailed a thumb and finger down one of the sharp lapels of Travis' suit jacket.

"Well, now he's doing more than just blackmailing me, Sir. Now he's doing more than just forcing me to do his assignments, and more than making me pay for clothes and men's jewelry for him, Sir," Travis blubbered on and on. "He, he makes me come to his dorm room, Sir, where he sometimes ties me to a chair while I'm wearing just my socks, Sir, and he makes me sit with a giant butt-plug or a vibrating dildo jammed up my hole. Sometimes he makes me go to his dorm room and he, uh, he…'

As Travis spoke, his lips quivered crazily and he found that he could not even get the next words out.

"He what???" Spike reeled and threw his half-smoked cigarette to the ground, inwardly knowing what Travis was about to say.

Travis looked down at the ground, his shoulders heaving up and down, tears flowing, and in a cracked and remorseful tone of voice, he croaked, *Please forgive me, Sir. It's not like I want to do it, it's not like I want him to do it to me, Sir. He fucks me, he rapes me, constantly, Sir, HE RAPES ME CONSTANTLY!!!"*

Then, without having been granted permission, Travis relieved his stance of attention and threw his huge football player sized arms around Spike and pulled the mangy guy close to him. As he shook and heaved against Spike, Travis went on saying, "And he's made it abundantly clear that if I don't do as he says all the time, he'll stream the video of me and you on the internet!"

Spike slowly wrapped his arms around the sobbing Travis as the football player shook and trembled even more and begged him, "Please, Sir, don't punish me for allowing him to have his liberties with me. I really have no choice, Sir. If that video goes on You Tube, my career will be finished before it's begun!"

"It's all right, bud, calm down," Spike whispered in Travis' ear, gently caressing the back of the jock boy's neck while running his hand over the soft textures of Travis' short hair, which was starting to grow back. "Don't think about this shit for another second, bud. I'll take care of that mother-fucker that you can take to your bank, for sure."

Travis slowly let go of Spike and resumed his stance.

"Sorry for blubbering like that, Sir, but I'm hurting real bad rectal-wise and," Travis began, but Spike held up a halting hand, cutting Travis' words off in mid-sentence.

"No need to go on," Spike said and tugged at Travis' tie. "Your right to speak is done for the moment."

"Sir, yes Sir," Travis said, and without another word, Spike walked off, his teeth clenched in an anger that even he had never felt before.

After a nearly two hour drive, Spike pulled his pick-up truck into the parking lot of the infamous sleazy bar called The Local. This bar was the same site where a certain horny (straight) sailor who was on leave from his ship once found himself tied up to a stall door in the men's room with his cock hanging out of the glory hole for all the sleazy, cock hungry patrons to milk all the live-long night. And milk that sailor they did, till his balls were drained and bone dry. The Local is also the sight where a handsome, muscular bank executive named Greg Smith found himself meanly stripped to his dress socks, tied to the stall door, and like the sailor, also milked till he thought he would lose his mind.

But now The Local would become the sight of John Broderick's punishment at the hands of Spike, along with some of his skinhead's buddies and other sleazy patrons of The Local. Spike stepped out of his pickup truck, then slammed the driver's side door shut and walked slowly toward the back section of the vehicle. At the sight of the huge laundry bag in the back of his pickup truck, with ropes tied tightly around it, Spike laughed uproariously.

"Hope you enjoyed the ride, asshole," Spike said and watched as the laundry bag squirmed and screaming came from within its confines. "Ha, never heard scummy laundry screaming like that before."

That said, Spike lowered the tailgate and hopped up into it, standing over the laundry bag.

"Okay, asshole, we've arrived where I intended to bring ya," Spike said and then bent down, undid the ropes around the bag and out popped John Broderick, bound and gagged.

John let out a muffled scream as he lay there in a blood-crusted mess, wearing nothing but a pair of black silk socks as he squirmed his way out of the bag, looking around in wonderment at where he had been taken.

"Now I'll tell ya, asshole, this place isn't as crowded in the afternoons as it is at night, but there's still enough clientele here to make your life as miserable as possible," Spike said as he reached down again and yanked the gag from John's mouth.

John railed through his bloody mouth, now missing four teeth, "You fucker, you kidnapped me!!! You can't do this!! I didn't do this to your jock pussy and—"

But John's words were cut off as Spike kicked him hard in the ribs, causing a spray of blood to foam out of the captive's mouth.

John reeled in pain as he pulled himself up to his knees, his head hanging down, gasping and heaving pitifully.

"You can avoid all that I plan to have done to you here at this place, you asshole," Spike ranted downward at the crying and trembling John. "All you got to do is tell me where the fuck the video is."

"Never!!! And I know you won't kill me, so go ahead and have your worst done. I'll tell you this, you mangy lowlife," John said with a sneer, his bloody mouth making him look all the more deranged. "Because if you kill me, you'll *never* find out where the video is. And when I do get back to my dorm room, I am going to stream it on the internet, and then Travis and his whole *fucking family* will be ruined beyond repair!"

"Naw, man, I won't kill ya," Spike said, then hauled John up and over his shoulders in a fireman's carry. "I'm gonna allow something worse than killing ya to be done to ya."

"Huh??? What in all fucks are you talking about, fuck-head???" John ranted as he was bounced along on Spike's shoulders toward the entrance of the sleazy bar. "What in all fucks could be worse than killing a guy???"

As Spike entered the bar a few moments later, catcalls and greetings were shouted at him. John knew in an instant that this was not a good place. Spike lugged John to the back of the dimly lit, cigarette and pot smoke smelling establishment and slammed him down on his back on the pool table.

John groaned as he lay there gasping, and then hands were set upon him.

He soon found his hands and feet were being tied to the four corners of the pool table.

"Jeez Louise, Spike, what'd you do to this mess of a guy?" a bald-headed barbarian asked the skinhead as he looked down at John spread open on the pool table, whimpering and whining miserably.

"Just warmed him up for *your* festivities, Leon," Spike said, then gave the bare-chested Leon's nipple ring a slight tug, sending a chill of elation through the giant of a guy. "I need some vital information out of this scumbag and I'm gonna let you and your buds here do whatever the fuck you want with him until he tells me what I want to know."

"I'll never tell! I'll fucking *never* tell you anything, dirt bag!" John railed over at Spike, his bloody mouth now looking more like a red hole in his head.

To shut John up, one of the leather-clad men reached down and backhanded him hard across the face, twice.

"You bastards!!" John screamed and was backhanded again.

Then, to his further horror and fear-stricken mind, John saw two video cameras being set up on the sides of the pool table.

"Wh—what the fuck???" John said and struggled against the bonds to no avail.

"Hey, seein' as you like videotaping guys in their private moments and then using those tapes as leverage against those guys, asshole, I just figured you would want a tape of your own, starring you, of course, to be shown to everyone, including your family, and your daddy, who's in prison," Spike said real snidely and lit a cigarette, his cock engorged in his mussed jeans as he watched John tremble and cry atop the pool table.

"I don't give a rat's ass," John responded. "Go ahead and stream me on the internet. Your waste of a jock pussy still gets his video shown on You Tube and—"

At the sound of John's slur against his special boy, Spike stepped loudly next to the pool table and grabbed a handful of the college guy's testicles, twisting them hard and squeezing the tar out of them.

"AAARRRHHHHHHHH!!!" John cried, arching his head back a bit as he was treated to a face-full of cigar smoke from the leather-clad men standing over him.

"We can start him off with this," Leon said to Spike as he held up a long and thick black latex dildo.

"S—start me off with that???" John reeled and struggled mightily against his bonds now, the pain in his testicles suddenly forgotten. "Fuck, no one can take something like that up their goddamned shit chute!!!"

Spike smiled maniacally down at John and said, "Aw, not to worry, asshole, we'll open you up slowly and methodically to make it fit."

John screamed when he saw the leather men gathering around the table greasing up their hands with Crisco shortening and opening and closing their hands in and out of big fists.

"We'll fist ya a few times real good to get that backdoor of yours open and accommodating for that big old nasty dildo's ride inside ya," an older leather man said to John, then leaned down and kissed the college boy on his bloody lips. "That way when we get to the *really* big dildos, it'll be like child's play for you to take 'em up the rear."

All the men laughed meanly as John cried, sniveled and sobbed.

"Action!!" Spike instructed and then two of the leather guys started inserting and extracting fingers, one and two and three and four at a time, in and out of John's hole, their shortening sopped fingers lubing and prepping him for the tortures to come.

"You bastards! Noooo, you can't, I'll sue this place!!" John threatened and gasped as his cock slowly grew hard and stiff.

It seemed that the sleazy and horned up patrons had suddenly doubled in number as they made their way to the pool table to get dibs on fingering the young college student's asshole.

"You can sue all you want, bud," Leon said as he held up the giant dildo for John to take a good look at. "But I'll tell ya this, college bud, when you do sue us and you tell the lawyer you hire where this place is, it won't exist, HARRRRRRR!!!"

Once more all the men laughed meanly as the men fingering John's rectal opening started being less gentle as they had been at first.

"NO, NO, NO, OH GOD, NO!!!" John blubbered and Spike punched the guy hard in the face again, just for the fuck of it.

"Where's the video, asshole???" Spike asked. "Tell me where the video is and all this stops!"

For good measure, Spike punched John again across the face, sending yet another tooth and more blood flying from his mouth.

"Fuck, but ya sure as all fucks can take it, I'll give ya that, man," Spike said.

"Do your worst! Do your goddamned worst!!" John bellowed crazily as his vision started to blur. "Because I will *not* tell you where the video is!!! And I plan to fuck your jock pussy boy every chance I get and—"

With that, Spike punched John, and the guy's cock spewed forth an uncontrollable mess of pent-up piss all over his upper torso.

The men cheered him on as they began sliding five fingers at a time into his stretching asshole, opening the college boy up more with each thrust.

"Oh God, don't, don't do this to me, dudes," John begged and looked at Spike meanly.

Suddenly, a twisted idea popped into John's mind.

"His, his pussy boy, his pussy boy is a real prince, a real handsome Prince Charming, a real fucking darling," John ranted upwards, grunting breathlessly as the guy with an unusually big hand was slowly slinking that big hand into his shit chute. "And I got the goods on that jock pussy boy; he'll do anything I say, including servicing you dudes. He would have to!!"

In response, the man with his hand now in John's shit chute looked up at the college boy incredulously and said, "Spike was right about

you, lowlife. You have no heart, but I say you got no soul either."
With that, the man twisted his hand into a fist inside John.

John screamed and nearly passed out.

To keep him awake and aware, John was suddenly treated to a nose-full of poppers.

"UHHHHHHH!!!!!" the college boy railed as one guy held his head tight and in place while another stuck two small bottles of poppers into his nostrils.

"Thanks, Leon. Eventually this stack of shit will tell me where the video is," Spike said.

"And if he don't, well, I'm sure as hell having a good time here," Leon said and held up the giant dildo.

He and Spike laughed meanly.

Then, when John's asshole had been stretched to the point that all the sleazy patrons of the bar approved, the college boy's legs were stretched even further apart so that his asshole was *truly* on display, gaping and wide open.

"Hope you're about ready for this now," Leon said and stood at the front of the pool table, directly between John's spread and upturned legs.

"Please, man, PLEASE, don't, I swear, I'll do anything you want," John pleaded.

"Tell my buddy, Spike, where that video is," Leon said.

"Anything except that!!" John railed and spat bloody phlegm at Leon.

Rage showed in Leon's eyes and he began thrusting the tip of the giant dildo into John's rectal cavity.

"Oh no, man! No!" John screamed as all the men hooted, hollered and cheered him on.

John's cock shriveled between his legs and beads of piss dripped from it.

The college boy cried and screamed in pain as the gargantuan dildo was slowly inserted into him.

"Now you'll know how my boy feels when he can't sit down for his classes," Spike whispered in John's ear and bit his earlobe just for the fuck of it.

9

It was now three hours after all the black skinheads had taken numerous turns fucking poor Bart Findley in his most private crevice. The golden boy of Calderfield College, in a daze, his asshole aching with an indescribable pain, was now alone in the sauna. Bart's head spun as he lay on the long, cushioned massage table, his hands now untied and his hugely muscular arms dangling off the sides of it, and his sock blindfold dangling around his neck. He inhaled the scents of the cooled down mineral rocks. Obviously the rocks had burnt out by then or the black skinheads planned to cook the jock later on. The room was filled with only the herbal, almost sickly scent of the mineral rocks. Bart tried to enjoy it as normally as possible, but *this* was no normal situation.

The football player lifted his head a bit and looked around the sauna. He took a deep breath, was able to smell the burnt out mineral rocks and the scent of them made his head spin and his vision blur. From what he could tell, he had been left alone after his horrendous ordeal.

Bart moaned miserably as his powerful arms and legs dangled off the sides of the table. His garters were torn and ruined, his navy blue sheer thick and thin socks half on and half off his big feet and his matching silk boxer briefs were gone, taken by one of the rapists as a twisted sort of souvenir of their conquest over him.

"Fuck, fuck, no one back at the college will ever believe this," Bart said to himself in misery as he swung his legs up to the tabletop and sat up on his elbows, breathing heavily. "How in all fucks am I going to get out of here??? I got no clothes whatsoever, shit!!! This has to be one of the sickest college tales that will *never* be told about. Gawd, but my poor shit chute hurts like the devil."

But then the scent from the sauna mineral rocks caused Bart's head to spin more and he slowly lay back down, sweating like a stuck pig atop the massage table. Bart's cock was soft and shriveled between his muscular legs. There was no way he could shoot another load, not after all the times he had cum involuntarily while being brutally jack-hammered and fucked by one black skinhead after the other. His testicles were aching just as much as his asshole, and his big, chewed up nipples were erect beyond reason.

"Dear God, please don't let those guys fuck me again," Bart whimpered as he twisted his head from side to side, then closed his eyes.

Visions of being fucked by two other people in his past filled his tortured mind.

As Bart drifted into a stupor, his asshole burned and he again recalled the night his own date with his physics classmate, Lisa; and then his unexpected date, not just with Lisa, but with her kinky and erotic-minded bisexual roommate, Karen.

"Lisa, Lisa, what in all hell???" Bart asked, pulling his mouth away from her nipple.

He was still bound to the headboard and unable to set himself free. "S—someone is massaging my goddamned feet, Lisa. What's going on here???"

"Just relax and enjoy it, Mr. Findley," Lisa said, sounding real sexy as she again slid her nipple into Bart's mouth. "Suck."

Bart did as he was told, looking up at Lisa in wonderment at the same time.

At his brown silk, sheer socked feet, Karen was gently massaging Bart's tootsies, her hands gripping them alternately and squeezing them tightly.

Bart swooned as he sucked heartily at Lisa's nipple, caressing it with the tip of his tongue, sending chills up and down her spine.

Lisa gripped the back of Bart's huge neck and pressed his mouth harder against her nipple.

"Nurse on me, Bart," Lisa whispered, but then the handsomer than handsome football player panicked again when he felt Karen winding a length of rope around one of his socked ankles.

Bart gasped and again pulled his mouth away from Lisa's nipple.

"Holy shit, why is whoever the fuck that is tying up my damned feet, Lisa?" Bart asked and craned his neck a bit to take in the sight of Karen as she worked most speedily at getting his first foot tied up.

She looped and wound the rope around his socked ankle as if her life depended on it. As he looked up at Lisa and saw the maniacal look in her eyes, he blurted, "Oh shit, shit, what do you two bitches have in mind for me???"

In response, Lisa trailed a finger under Bart's chin, fed her nipple back into his mouth, and said, "Suck."

While he was sort of terrified over not knowing what Lisa and Karen had planned for him, another part of Bart was also mysteriously and somewhat erotically excited, and his huge erection was testament to both facts. Bart found himself growing fear-hard between his legs.

The football player crooned as he sucked, suckled and nursed like a madman on Lisa's tits, all the while Karen was binding up his big feet with mounds upon mounds of rope.

A short while later Bart Findley found himself bound to Lisa's bed in a most mortifying and heinous position. Every sexy part of his glorious musculature was on total display. With his arms still bound straight out against the headboard, his wrists locked in the leather restraints, Bart's feet had now been stretched to the sides of the bed and hoisted a bit upwards by the ropes that Karen had so expertly looped and wound about them. The ends of the ropes around his socked feet were tied off to the ends of the headboard as well, hence not only Bart's muscular body was on display, but his bunghole was very visible as well.

"Lisa, what in all hell is the point of all this???" Bart reeled, his hands curled into fists in the restraints as he squirmed.

"Me and my roommate want to have some lighthearted, deep-assed fun with you," Lisa replied, sounding snidely sexy and very mean at the same time.

"D—deep assed fun??? What the fuck does that mean?" Bart thundered, swinging his head from side to side, watching miserably as the two young women worked at getting him bound well to the headboard.

"Does this answer your question, Hercules?" Karen said as she tugged on her end of the rope. Bart's butt cheeks were lifted higher yet, putting his bunghole on bigger display.

"Oh fuck, I don't think I need three guesses to know what you two vixens are up to here," Bart reeled. Try as he might, he could not get himself loose from his bonds. "Shit, this is not my thing, you bitches!!!"

"Hmm, no respect at all," Karen said. "Looks like you need to learn a lesson, Mr. Findley.

That said, Karen finished tying her end of the rope around Bart's feet to the headboard.

Once Bart was securely bound, he watched as Karen opened a dresser drawer and took out a large, rectangular box.

"Would you care for a blindfold, Mr. Findley?" Karen asked, grinning meanly at the captive football player as she held up the box. "I have them in silk, leather, cotton and an array of colors that you can choose from as well."

"Fuck blindfolding me, what all are you two planning to do to me???" Bart reeled. "Fuck, but I'm totally on naked display here in just my damned socks!!"

"Yes, and what a display it is at that," Karen mused and held the box out for Lisa to open. "Would you do the honors, darling?"

"Certainly," Lisa replied and snapped the box open.

"Lisa, untie me, please don't let her," Bart began, but when he saw Lisa hold up a long pink latex, semi-thick dildo, he stopped his tirade in its tracks. "Oh holy shit!"

Bart was railing a few minutes later as the two women were now seated on the bed between his spread legs. Each of them were holding a small plastic bottle of strawberry scented lubricant in their hands. They sloshed and sluiced the lubricant onto their fingers and then squeegeed their lube sopped fingers into the tied up football player's hole.

"Oh God, quit that, you two, huh?" Bart pleaded.

"It's so tight in there, yes?" Karen asked Lisa.

"I guess that's why they call him a tight-end," Lisa said, then laughed and slid two of her lube drenched fingers into Bart's anal opening, his hole squeezing around them as she prodded and drenched his ass walls.

"Bitch, that's what you are, Lisa! I'm not a tight end, I'm a god-damned quarterback," Bart said, then suddenly screeched in ecstasy as Lisa dug her fingers deeper inside him.

In no time, he shot his load.

"Oh my lord, he's the type that cums when his ass is porked," Karen said enthusiastically. "Okay, let's finish lubing him and then start diddling him with dildos. I want to see how much sperm this studly footballer has in those big balls of his."

"Aw no, no, no you bitches, you wouldn't," Bart begged miserably as Lisa extracted her fingers from his hole and Karen quickly slid hers in, the smell of strawberry lube starting to become overbearing.

When Bart's hole was as wet as a duck's back and sticky as fly-paper, the two young women began taking turns slowly inserting dildos of various sizes, lengths, widths and colors into his gaping anal opening. The squishing sounds as the dildos entered him was maddening for the handsome jock. More maddening, however, was the feeling of the dildos as they kissed his ass walls and teased his sphincter. And every time the dildos kissed his sphincter, Bart felt his balls churning and cooking up hefty loads of sperm.

"Oh Gawd, why are you two doing this to me???" Bart asked.

"How could we not?" Karen said as she slid a rather large dildo into Bart's hole.

"Oh no, not again, bitches!! You two are getting my nut here!!" Bart reeled, his eyes crossed, making the two young women giggle loudly.

He shot his load a second time, all over his upper torso.

As Bart shot his load like a madman, Karen slowly thrust the dildo in and out of his hole. This made the football player's head spin even more, and made his hole hypersensitive. As Karen held her dildo buried in Bart's hole, she leaned over, kissed Lisa on the lips and said, "It's a known fact that if a guy has something wedged in his hole while and after he shoots his load, it makes his hole all the more susceptible.

"No shit Sherlock," Bart fumed.

When Karen slid her dildo out of Bart's hole, Lisa wasted no time in sliding another, wider one in. "Aw Gawd, Lisa, no!!!"

Bart squirmed miserably on the globes of his ass as Lisa wedged and twisted her latest dildo into him.

"No, Lisa, please, give a dude a break here, huh?" Bart pleaded.

He arched his head back and rolled his eyes in his head as Lisa fucked his hole with her dildo as Karen leaned down over his semi-hard, sensitive feeling cock and gobbled it into her mouth.

The two women had a ball watching Bart suffer in the throes of forced ecstasy.

"Oh, my buds'll never believe this," Bart said as the dildo slithered deeper and deeper into his bowels. "Sexy bitches, you two are."

As his asshole was dildoed and his cock was sucked, Bart was able to feel his balls cooking up another hefty helping of football player sperm.

"Oh, oh fuck, oh you bitches from hell," Bart panted, looking down and watching in awe as Karen worked her mouth magic on his tingling cock. "I can't believe this, but I can feel it, you two are gonna make me spill my seed again."

"Go for it," Karen said with a grin, holding Bart's throbbing cock in hand and grinning at him, pre-cum dripping on the sides of her lips.

When Lisa slammed her dildo deep inside Bart, he yelped loudly that he was about to "fucking cum" again. Karen slurped his cock back into her mouth and the football player fed her his sperm. Screaming in a man's passion as he did so, Bart ranted about how he was cumming again and so soon at that, cumming again and again.

"Cumming, I'm cumming again," Bart panted now in the sauna

as he slowly climbed out of the heat induced stupor he had fallen victim to a short twenty minutes ago.

As Bart awoke in the sauna he was suddenly aware of the fact that what he was feeling in his cock this time was no dream or memory, because this time his cock was being sucked, but not be a sexy college student named Karen, his cock was being sucked by a black skinhead who seemed fixated on getting a load out of the captive football player.

"UHHHHH," Bart grunted as he sat up on his elbows once more atop the massage table. "Wh—who are you?"

"You can call me Lionel, I'll just call you whatever the fuck comes to mind, white boy," the thin black guy wearing just a pair of ankle length red sweat socks said to Bart, then sucked the football player's sore cock back into his mouth.

Realizing that the sauna device had been turned off, Bart said, "Yeah, somehow I knew you would, Lionel. Easy with my cock, huh, man? I haven't had an easy time of it down here the last couple of days."

In response, Lionel simply sucked Bart's cock harder.

"Oh, got to admit that feels amazing. Say, Lionel, after you get me off, you suppose you can scare up some clothes so I can get the fuck out of here?" Bart asked, feeling himself about to shoot a dry load. "Fuck, man, help me, I want to get the fuck out of here already!!! Oh shit, I'm cumming again! Fucking shooting my load again!"

10

While Bart Findley was having his sore, spent cock brutally sucked by a black skinhead named Lionel, John Broderick was now screaming in mortal pain as Leon had the giant dildo wedged half-way inside him. Unlike Bart, who had derived some pleasure from what Lisa and Karen had done to him dildo-wise, John was deriving no pleasure whatsoever at what was being done to him.

"Oh god, man, oh god!!!" John roared as Spike smoked a cigarette and allowed the ashes to land on the tied down college boy's chest. "C'mon man, I feel like I'm being split in two here!! There is no fucking way he'll get that whole thing in me!! Ohhhhhhhhh!!!"

"Then tell me what the fuck I want to know, you lowlife black-mailer," Spike said calmly as Leon thrust the dildo further inside John's bowels.

John screamed.

"Fucker, you are, I never fucked the jock pussy this way, *never!!*" John pleaded.

Spike reached down and backhanded John across the face.

John screamed out again in pain.

"And you'll never fuck him again, trust me on that, you scumbag," Spike said and backhanded the blackmailer again. Now, I suggest you listen to me and listen closely, dirt bag, because I'm at the end of my rope with you here. I will say that you're a tough customer. God knows, I've knocked out a few of your teeth; no doubt you got some bruised and broken ribs there, your face is all bloodied and smacked up lookin' and you sure are shaved like a cue ball for this pool table. But now I want the video!!"

That said, Spike held up a hand to stop Leon from forcing the humungous dildo any further into John's rectum.

"Oh God, thank you, man, thank you," John whimpered and then looked up stupidly as Spike held up a rubber band. "Fuck, now what? What do you plan to do with that???"

In answer to his question, Spike tied the rubber band a few times around John's nut sac.

"Oh fuck, what are you going to do to me now???" John cried, spittle flying from his mouth as he looked frantically at the video cameras at his sides.

"Okay John, you dick, you fucking lower than scum lowlife, I am going to cut your nuts off," Spike said as he reached into the pocket of his jeans and brought out his knife, the same knife he had once terrorized Travis with. "You won't die after I castrate you because my buddy Leon here was a medic in the army back in the day. He will seal the cut. You'll still have a dick, you dick, but no balls. Think about it, you lowlife, trashy bastard! What are you, twenty-one, twenty-two...twenty-three at most??? Think about it, no balls for the rest of your pathetic life!"

"No, no, you just don't get it, man, the jock pussy, his dad, his dad ruined my," John panted, but Spike clamped a hand over his mouth, silencing him in mid-sentence.

"Hey, lemme tell you, lowlife, I don't give a rat's ass what Travis' dad did to your dad," Spike went on. "That ain't my issue. That's for the courts and the high socked lawyers to decide on. And you dragged my boy into it. I bet he had no idea what the fuck you were blackmailing him for. You really think he deserved that??? Now, I want the video, and if there's more than one, I want that one, too. And like I said, any copies you might have made of it! I want all of them!!!"

With that, Spike swung his knife through the air and John screamed.

"Don't fuck with me, lowlife. I'm tired of dealing with you today. I'm tired of looking at you," Spike said as he pressed the tip of his knife against the skin of John's shaved nut sac.

"Oh God. No, please, man, no!!" John screamed in a high crescendo.

Spike moved the knife to John's pubic area and slightly cut into the skin.

John screamed out, "Okay, okay, okay! I'll give you the video! I'll give you the video!!!" and then pissed long and hard all over the pool table.

Leon slowly extracted the oversized dildo from John's asshole and Spike put his knife back in his pocket.

"Where is it?" Spike asked and John could see that the man meant business.

"I—I'll get it for you when we get back to my dorm room, man," John said as he sniveled miserably.

"If you're fucking with me," Spike said, reaching toward his pocket where the knife was.

"No, no, I swear, I'm telling you the truth. I'll give you the videos. I just want to get out of here and maybe get to a doctor and a dentist, too," John whimpered and all the sleazy patrons of The Local laughed uproariously at his patheticness.

Spike reached down and undid the ropes around John's right wrist as Leon undid the ones around his left wrist.

"Go to the men's room and gather yourself together," Spike said to John, who sat up and undid the ropes around his feet himself. He hopped off the pool table and, shaking from head to toe, limped to the men's room.

"Don't you think he might try to go out the window in there and get away from you, Spike?" Leon asked.

"And go where in just his socks?" Spike asked. "Plus, we're a million miles from nowhere. He came here in a goddamned laundry bag, he has no clue where we are. No, he ain't goin' out a window."

"And knowing you, you're taking him back in the laundry bag," Leon said with a laugh.

Spike simply nodded.

In the men's room, John took in the sight of the stall with the glory hole cut in the door. The blackmailer knew of the urban legend of a hot sailor boy who had supposedly once spent hours standing in that stall, tied to the stall door with his cock and balls sticking out of the glory hole for all the patrons of the bar to suck and steal his cum. Like him, the sailor boy had been stripped to his dress socks.

John stepped to the sink, ran the water and washed the blood from his mouth, spitting over and over. Shaking in his socks, he also thought of the numerous plights of a hunky bank executive named Greg Smith, who had supposedly spent time tied up in that stall with his manly package on display in the glory hole as well. John's asshole burned, his mouth and jaws were swollen to three times their normal size and he was as bald as an eagle, yet his cock pounded long and hard between his legs as he thought of the perils of the men who had experienced the infamous glory hole at The Local. John knew of The Local and the legends attached to it, and he also thought how it would have been so awesome to have subjected Travis O' Toole the fourth to the glory hole. The thought of Travis standing there tied to that stall door, naked but for a pair of sheer socks with his trademark garters thrown in just for the fuck of it; his huge nine inch cock and big balls sticking out of the glory hole made John's cock engorge all the more. But now, that wasn't meant to be, unless he wanted to lose his own balls in the process.

John Broderick realized that he was suffering between a mixture of pleasure and pain, and the feeling was fueling new and more clever thoughts of how he could at last get to the root of his dad's predicament and possibly get him sprung from prison on the trumped up charges that Travis' dad had manufactured. With a fat lipped bloody grin, John mused to himself, "Travis O' Toole the third..." and looked again at the glory hole.

About ten minutes later, John emerged from the stall after relieving himself, shaking like a leaf as he sat on the shitter; and not only had he relieved himself, but he had also jacked himself off two times in heated succession thinking of how he would enlist some help in getting his dad out of prison.

When John emerged from the bathroom, still looking beaten and forlorn, he slowly made his way over to the pool table where Spike was waiting with the huge laundry bag.

"Say, man, can't you just get me some damned clothes to wear for the ride back to the campus?" John asked as the skinhead blew cigarette smoke in his face. "I mean, being stuffed in a goddamned laundry bag isn't my idea of a good time."

But then, John's words were cut short as Spike, moving faster than the eye could see and sucker punched him right in the gut.

John grunted, doubled over, gripped his mid-section and was then treated to a hard conk on the top of his head, courtesy of Spike as well.

John hit the floor hard at Spike's booted feet and lay in a pain-filled stupor.

Standing nearby, Leon grinned from ear to ear.

"You sure know how to handle the bad boys, Spike," Leon said as he came over and assisted Spike in getting the blackmailer stuffed into the laundry bag.

"Yeah, and from now on I'll know how to handle the good boys as well. One in particular, that is," Spike said as visions of Travis flitted through his mind. "My fuckin' angel."

A short while later, Leon was waving from the entrance of The Local as Spike drove off in his pick-up truck with Jon in the back. As Leon waved with one hand, he held in his other hand the pair of black silk socks that John had been wearing, the souvenir gift that Spike had bestowed on his good buddy for his twisted assistance in the matter of the video.

Leon wandered back into The Local grinning from ear to ear as he watched the owners, Alex and Ronald, guiding a muscular, blind-folded and naked sailor toward the men's room.

The sailor's hands were tied tightly behind him; his cock was huge and engorged between his legs thanks to a dose of Viagra. The sailor grimaced miserably and demanded that he finally be allowed to return to his ship. Instead, he was taken into the men's room blubbering miserably as he was tied to the stall door with the glory hole cut in it and his cock and balls stuck through the hole. He heard one of his captors say, "Its feeding time at The Local, Sailor boy."

* * *

A couple of hours later, Spike was back in John's dorm room with the blackmailer, dumping him unceremoniously from the laundry bag. John came out of the bag totally naked, hands tied behind his back and gagged.

He snarled as he hit the floor.

Spike squatted down and used his knife to undo the ropes bidning John's hands.

"Get on your feet, lowlife, and *get me the video!!*" Spike reeled as he stood up straight.

Prying the foul tasting bandanna gag from his mouth, John did as he was told and dashed over to his bed. Spike watched as John reached under and between the mattress and bedspring.

"Typical, why didn't I think of that?" Spike asked with a grin.

A few seconds later, John was holding out two DVDs.

"Nah man, play 'em for me first," Spike said with total authority. "I want to be sure of what you're giving me here."

John turned towards the small entertainment center in his room and used a remote control to turn on the DVD player and TV set.

Moments later, Spike watched the DVD with a feeling of rage and total wrath. He watched as Travis was humiliated by him and sucked his cock. This was the man he had come to call not just his jock pussy, but his angel. Standing next to him, feeling totally vulnerable in his nakedness and pain, John Broderick watched as well.

"I should fucking kill you for this, asshole," Spike fumed, then grabbed John by one arm and produced his knife yet again.

"No, no, you said if I gave you the video," John pleaded as Spike moved behind him and held the knife directly under his balls.

John started crying pathetically, then lost control and pissed right onto Spike's boots.

"I knew it, you lowlife, you want my boots, too!" Spike jeered and pulled the knife away from John's balls. "But no fucking way would I let you lick my damned boots! And now that your poison piss has been on them, I'm throwin' these shit kickers away!!"

"Look, you got what you came for, man. Just take the DVDs and leave, huh?" John pleaded as Spike inspected the second DVD, which was simply a copy of the original.

"Nah, man, you still got more stuff that I want," Spike said, then reached down and picked up the laundry bag in which he had transported John in and tossed it at him. "I want every stitch of clothing that you made my jock pussy buy for you, and that includes socks and underpants and any men's jewelry. And when I show it all to him, if everything he got for you ain't there, well, I'll be back, asshole!"

At that, John began packing the bag with all of what Spike had demanded.

As John packed, he watched as Spike dropped the two DVDs on the floor and crushed them to pieces under the heels of his piss soaked boots. The sounds and sight of the DVDs being destroyed filled John with woe.

"Gimme your cell phone, asshole," Spike said when John was finished packing the clothing and jewelry that Travis had purchased for him in the laundry bag. "The cell phone that you ain't supposed to even have, seeing as my jock pussy did mention that you had used the camera on your cell phone to catch that award winning video of me and him."

"Wh—why do you want my damned cell phone?" John asked.

Spike simply grinned.

"How stupid do you think I am, asshole?" Spike said, then reached downward and gave John's balls a good hard squeeze and twist.

"Yow!!" John screamed. "Oh, my balls, man!"

"Get me your cell phone, asshole, and God help you if you have more than one and I find out about it, because, believe me, you'll be making a return trip to The Local, and this time I *will* cut off these nuts of yours," Spike said and released his hold on John's balls and thrust the guy backward.

John stumbled in his nakedness, but quickly balanced himself.

Seconds later, the blackmailer watched as Spike did the same thing to his cell phone that he had done to the DVDs.

"The way I heard it, cell phones ain't permitted on this campus," Spike said through clenched teeth.

"That's a goddamned stupid rule, man, and I swear that I deleted the video from my phone," John panted miserably.

"You don't like the rules of the college, asshole," Spike said as he picked up the laundry bag, "then leave. The way I see it, no one wants you here anyway. And do I give a shit if you deleted the video or not? This way I know it's been deleted for fucking ever!"

Spike sneered as he opened the door to John's dorm, and in parting, said, "And if I hear from my jock pussy that you're harassing him, or even talking to him, or if you even look at him—"

"I won't, I won't," John blubbered, standing there naked and mortified and praying that no one passed by in the hall as Spike stood in the open doorway.

Spike spit on the floor of John's dorm room and then walked out, slamming the door behind him and taking the laundry bag full of Travis' belongings with him.

Once Spike was gone, John locked the door to his room and headed for the shower.

As he let the warm water soothe his battered, bald body, the black-mailer grinned and said to himself, "No, I won't go near Travis O' Toole the fourth ever again. I admit I learned my lesson there and learned from my mistake as well. But I will be making a visit to Travis O' Toole the third very, very soon."

As John showered and thought of Travis' dad, he grabbed his cock and began stroking.

11

"OOOOOOOHHHH…UHHHHHHH!!!   GAWWWWDDD!!!"
Bart Findley grunted, gurgled and gasped as yet another dry load
was forced from him courtesy of the black skinhead, Lionel, who
was currently sucking his cock.

Lionel grinned meanly down at Bart as he lay atop the massage
table in the sauna at the gym.

"How many times that make now, white boy?" Lionel asked as he
leered at Bart while holding the football player's shriveled cock in
his big hand, teasing the tip of it with the pad of his thumb.

"UHHHHH…I—I don't, man, I lost count a while back," Bart
panted, gasping for breath and rubbing the heels of his ruined blue
sheer socks against the end of the table.

As his spent cock was squeezed and teased, Bart gripped the sides
of the massage table with his huge hands and pleaded to Lionel.
"Please, man, please, help me, get me outa here. I'm so fucking
scared that all those other dudes are gonna come back and ream my
asshole again and I don't think I can take that again…AND…OHH-
HHHHH FUUUUCCCKKKK!!!!!!"

Bart gripped the sides of the table even tighter as Lionel grabbed
him by his socked ankles, moved him downward till the football
player's asshole was on total display, and spread his legs real wide.

"Yo don't need to be worryin' none about those homeboys comin'
back to have at this sweet hole of yours, white boy, at least not for
the next few hours," Lionel said with a laugh and aimed his huge,

rock hard cock at Bart's open back doorway. "For now, it's just gonna be me and yous in this little hotel room of ours."

"You fucker," Bart reeled as his hole was entered and spread again.

"That is right, white boy, the walls of yo hole feel like sweet velvet to my cock, ah man, fuckin' beautiful white boy you are," Lionel quipped, gripping Bart's ankles tighter and plowing his way in.

"I'll kill you bastards for this, swear that I will," Bart whispered and as he was fucked yet again.

Much to his disbelief, his balls churned and his sore and over-used cock engorged.

Bart seethed, thinking how this was worse, much worse than what Lisa and her twisted roommate, Karen, had once done to him anally.

As Bart was fucked by Lionel, his mind wandered back again to what he had come to call his fateful date.

"Lisa, Lisa, listen to me, please. Like any other dude, I love shootin' my damned load; I even love *being made* to shoot my load," Bart said crazily. "But what I'm truly *not* enjoying here is having you and whatever the fuck your roomie's name is shoving those damned dildos from hell up my shit chute!!"

In response, Lisa simply slid the thick, pink latex dildo that was currently wedged inside the handsome, sweating football player out and Karen once more began sloshing his hole with strawberry scented lube.

"If you're not enjoying it, then why do you cum like crazy while being porked?" Karen asked teasingly.

Looking down at his cum soaked chest, a feeling of erotic humiliation engulfed Bart.

"I don't know, bitch, and that ain't for you to know either," Bart railed and again shook his wrists in the restraints holding him to the bed. "No one asked you to find out about whatever weakness I have. Now I demand that you release me and fucking *quit* feeding me that strawberry shit through my anal canal, huh???"

Lisa giggled and said, "I just love how macho you are when you're pissed off, Mr. Findley."

"Oh yeah, well, I'll tell you, Lisa, when it comes to me being pissed off, you haven't seen anything yet!" Bart replied and then swooned as she and Karen took turns again teasing his sopped up hole with their fingers.

"Oh fuck, I swear, when I'm outa these bonds you two got me in, I'm gonna wreak havoc on both of you," Bart cried.

"No you're not," Karen said. "When you're out of those bonds you're going to ask us when the next time will be when we can do this to you again."

Then she and Lisa extracted their fingers from Bart's hole and held up a plastic funnel.

"We'll just see about that and, *holy fuck,* what now???" Bart screamed as Karen inserted the stem-end of the funnel into the football player's rectal hole and Lisa began pouring a vial of clear liquid into him.

Bart could feel whatever it was being fed to him sluicing through his innards.

"Wh—what all is that you're feeding me ass-wise?" Bart asked incredulously.

"It's a special potion that I found on the internet, it comes from the Orient. It's used there to help studly men like you along even after they've cum a few times. It keeps their ladies very happy," Karen said, then she and Lisa laughed meanly. "We want to be sure that you're like the Energizer bunny rabbit, Bart Findley."

"Yeah, he kept going and going, but because of you two and your twisted antics, I'm gonna keep cumming and cumming. OH, MY FUCKING NERVES, you bitches."

When the vial was empty, Lisa tossed it aside and she and her roommate took in the sight of the hulking football player tied to their dorm room bed as he squirmed in the tight bindings.

"Hoooo Gawd, I can feel it already," Bart panted as his sore cock began tingling.

The two young women smiled ravenously at him and they each reached for another dildo.

"Awwww no, wouldn't you two bitches from hell prefer taking turns riding my hard cock rather than squeezing fake ones in and out of me???"

"We have all night, Mr. Findley," Karen laughed and began inching a thick purple dildo into Bart's stretched hole.

Bart breathed in deeply, clenched his restrained hands into big meaty fists and sneered at his two kinky captors.

"Bitches! Feels so good, though, the way my cock plumps up," Bart sputtered.

The two young women looked at each other and smiled triumphantly.

"I told you this would be great fun," Karen said to Lisa and slid the purple dildo further inside Bart.

Karen slid the dildo in and out of Bart's rectum, teasing him meanly with it. It took longer for him to grow erect this time, despite the liquid potion streaming through him. Lisa cuddled up next to Bart as Karen methodically slid the dildo just about all the way inside Bart. As Lisa kissed him on the lips, sucked his earlobes, kissed his cheeks and eyelids, Karen slid the dildo out, and back in repeatedly.

"Oh, fucking bitches, making me crazier than crazy," Bart reeled.

Lisa knew in her heart of hearts that the so-called potion that they had pumped into Bart ass-wise was nothing more than some edible scented lube mixed with over the counter liquid vitamins, totally harmless stuff. She had fallen for this guy really hard and she was not about to allow any harm to come to him whatsoever. But teasing him psychologically really was having an enormous effect on his cock. It was amazing what the body could do when one was being psychologically teased.

Then, a short while later, as Karen was sliding a black and very thick dildo inside Bart, he felt his nuts churning again, cooking up another load of slop, he was sure.

"UHHH, fucking bitches, this load is gonna be one for the history books," Bart grunted as Lisa was busily sucking one of his earlobes.

"What with how many times I've already splattered my mess on my chest here, with that goddamned potion of potency you fed me ass-wise, fuck, I'm cumming, cumming, and cumming like a madman!!"

Bart bucked in his bonds, writhed like crazy on the bed as his muscular body became a mass of goose bumps.

The football player roared from deep in his throat, his sperm spewing like a faucet out of his piss hole.

As he seemed to cum relentlessly, Bart felt as if he was literally a man possessed.

Karen slid the dildo halfway in him and it was music to the vixen's ears when she heard Bart demand, "Fucking bitch, bury that thing inside me, fuck, there's more of my good stuff aching to get out."

And Karen did just that and she and Lisa laughed meanly as Bart shot his load.

"After a few more helpings of my secret potion from the Orient, he'll be ready for our pussies," Karen said and then slid the black dildo halfway out of the football player.

"Aw, no, no!" Bart was crying a few scant moments later, his entire body feeling beyond sensitized.

"Aw no, no," Bart muttered in the sauna after having been ass-fed Lionel's creamy sperm.

"You said something, white boy?" Lionel asked, then sauntered over to the steaming mineral rocks and poured some hot water over them.

The hiss of steam was instantaneous and Bart slowly lifted his head from the massage table. As Lionel stood facing the mineral rocks, watering them through the steam in the sauna, Bart took in the sight of one of the most beautifully shaped asses he had ever seen. The football player's eyes roamed over Lionel's muscular thighs, up to a pair of ass mounds that looked like two smooth, hard coconuts hanging next to each other.

"Oh holy shit, better ass than a woman," Bart said to himself as he licked his lips hungrily.

As Lionel bent down to scratch an itch on his leg, his asshole was suddenly exposed between his sexy, well-muscled ass cheeks.

"Like a goddamned pussy hole, only no doubt tighter, holy fuck, " Bart whispered, amazed to find himself attracted to this man.

As Lionel rose back to his feet, his big balls swung between his legs.

"Just fixing it so you cook some more in here, white boy, before the next round of all that ass action you been enjoyin' so much," Lionel said, his back still to Bart as he fired up the mineral rocks. Through the haze of the steam engulfing him, Bart grinned and thought, you don't know me all that well, my skin-headed bud. I ain't known as the Calderfield College Golden Boy for nothing. No way, I'm hard as gold, and with a spent cock and in no time at that. Heh, and me thinks it's time that *you* knew the feeling of something big, thick and long being rammed up your ass, or in your case, Lionel, your sweet lookin' pussy hole that you got there between those coconut-like ass mounds of yours. Oh fuck, yeah...

With that in mind, Bart sat halfway up on the massage table, his sore cock hard and tingling between his muscular, tree trunk-like legs, ready to hop down off the table and plow his erection into the sweet pussy hole of the black skinhead.

But to Bart's dismay, as he sat up, he realized that his hands were once more bound tightly behind him, and the slack of the rope was tied off to the sides of the massage table, holding the football player firmly in place.

"Aw, holy fuck, you play dirty, Lionel. Fucking bastard tied me the fuck up again," Bart mumbled, then fell back onto the table in a prone position, his engorged cock sticking up like a flagpole. As he squirmed in the forced ecstasy, Lionel approached the table, a shit eating grin on his sadistic face.

"You all said something, white boy, Mr. Football dee-lite?" Lionel teased, then stepped to the side of the table, leaned down and slurped Bart's hard, sweaty cock into his mouth for another go-round.

"Fucker," Bart wailed. As he arched his handsome head back, the steam of the sauna cooking him made his head spin into a new reverse orbit as Lionel chowed on him yet again. "Teaser, you knew that the sight of your sexy black man rear end and pussy hole would enflame my poor spent cock!! I must have been totally zoned out when you tied me the fuck up again like this. Dirty pool!"

As Lionel snickered meanly with Bart's cock deep in his throat, the football player felt his aching balls churning and cooking up a dry load that would send him to heights he'd never known before. Or perhaps, he thought, heights even higher than that of what Lisa and Karen had sent him on.

As Lionel sucked and teased Bart's stiff cock, Bart's mind wandered back again to the night of his date with Lisa and his forced date with her roommate, Karen.

After he shot his secret potion induced load all over his chest, stomach and nipples, the football player found himself in a state of heightened ecstasy that he had never before known. The two young women untied one of his big socked feet and stretched him out on the bed, leaving his wrists locked in the restraints on the headboard.

Bart wailed as tears of anger, exhaustion and ecstasy streamed from his eyes.

"Fucking bitches sure know how to use and abuse a poor football player, I gotta say. My asshole sure is smarting right about now," Bart seethed.

The two young women giggled and snuggled up on either side of the still bound Bart Findley.

"So, you're not pissed with me, Mr. Findley?" Lisa asked, then gently pecked Bart on the cheek.

"Pissed? I'm anything but," Bart replied, taking deep breaths and smiling from ear to ear. "This has to be the craziest date I've ever been on."

"Well, it's about to get even crazier," Karen said, and then snickered and grabbed Bart's spent cock and squeezed it meanly.

"Owwwww!! Hey, you sick bitch!! That's my cock, lady!!!" Bart thundered.

While his mouth was wide open, Lisa did the honors of squirting two blasts of the secret erection potion into it.

"There you go, Mr. Findley," Lisa teased.

Bart looked angrily over at Lisa, but before he could spit out the not-all-that-bad-tasting liquid, she grabbed his nose and chin and forced his mouth shut. Bart involuntarily swallowed.

"What was that you just forced me to swallow?" Bart asked miserably. "More secret potion, you bitches from hell????"

"Turns out he is pissed with us after all," Karen teased, then leaned over Bart's muscular torso, licked some of the cum off him and kissed Lisa on the lips.

Watching this spectacle caused Bart's sore cock to plump up yet again.

"Fuck, fuck, I love girl on girl action, and I love girl on girl action on me as well," Bart said, grinning and aching to fuck. "You two bitches can keep me here all night, no worries."

"Good, because we plan to do just that, muscle boy," Karen said snidely, then sucked Bart's caked up cum off one of his nipples.

She then leaned across to kiss Lisa again, feeding her roommate Bart's cum.

"Mmm," Lisa crooned as she and Karen made a real show of kissing and sucking his cum off him and feeding it to each other via kisses.

"You two are driving me insane," Bart murmured as he squirmed against his bonds. "I don't need three more guesses to know what you two are prepping me for now."

Lisa and Karen ate Bart's cum off his chest till his cock was hard as steel, the feeling of their lips and tongues devouring him and sucking his nipples every few seconds caused that erection.

Twenty minutes later, Bart was roaring in an animal-like passion, grunting, sweating and swearing like a captured marine as Lisa went first riding his hard cock, swaying back and forth on it, driving the football player mad with pleasure.

"Yeah, ride my cock, you bitch, ride my fucking spent cock. Feels so painfully awesome," Bart called out as he squeezed his eyes shut. "Fucking bitches from hell, best two things that ever happened to me, yeah!"

Then, when Bart opened his eyes, Karen was riding his cock, and then Lisa, and then Karen again. As he grunted and fucked for all he was worth, Bart's head spun. It was as if he was fucking both of the young women at the same time.

He shot his load that time deep inside Lisa as Karen gently squeezed his balls.

Lisa made sweet, orgasmic sounds as Bart gasped. Their sounds of passion was music to each other's ears as they came and came.

They rounded out their kinky romp a short while later. Once Bart was free from the restraints, he and Lisa each sucked one of Karen's nipples as she lay on the bed between them. They also took turns teasing her pussy with the now washed dildos that she and Lisa had used on Bart.

"So, you're sure you're not pissed with me, Mr. Findley?" Lisa asked as she and Bart teased Karen's pussy with a dildo each and Karen moaned in passion.

Bart smiled his killer smile and said, "Let's just say that if you and this bitch from hell don't tie me the fuck up again real soon and work me over, then I'll be really pissed."

All three of the college students laughed.

Bart's thoughts returned to the present again, and his memory and thoughts of Lisa and Karen faded as he shot his umpteenth dry load down Lionel's throat.

Fucking fuck, my night with Lisa and Karen turned out okay, Bart thought. "But how in all fucks will this turn out???

With that thought in mind, Bart panted and gyrated on the tabletop and swore once more as he shot a dry load, which nearly made him crazy.

Bart's cock tingled in Lionel's mouth as his orgasm consumed him, and eventually, Bart floated into a stupor of sorts.

As he lay there, he heard Lionel say to someone, "We need to get him out of here. At this point, if he's found like this, we could all be in trouble for kidnapping this side of beef."

Then Bart felt hands lifting him from the table, hands undoing the ropes around his wrists behind him and he was then lugged between a few of the black skinheads out of the sauna.

12

A few hours after Spike had retrieved and destroyed the DVDs, Spike was glad to find his angel hanging out at the Cherry Hill Mall food court with his golden haired suit buddy, Steve Schwartz. Steve sat with Travis in the food court, looking angelic and princely handsome, but not nearly as captivating as Travis. Spike sauntered slowly over to sit near where they were seated. He didn't want Travis to see him yet, he was more interested to know what his pussy boy's state of mind was, and the best way to learn that was to spy on him for just a bit.

As Spike sat down at a table a few feet from where Travis and Steve were seated, both of them enjoying a designer coffee and a light snack, the skin took in the fact that Travis was smartly dressed in a classic dark blue suit, a white shirt, burgundy tie, well-shined black lace-up wingtips and, of course, silk blue socks. Spike snickered a bit as he pictured the garters that were more than definitely clipped to those socks.

"Fuckin' jock pussy," Spike thought and refrained from smoking lest Travis smell the smoke and know he was there.

Steve Schwartz was dressed in a light brown, almost beige, suit, with a white shirt open at the neck, no tie, brown shoes and beige socks. The way Steve's socks were scrunched around his calves, Spike knew he was not sporting garters like his jock pussy. Steve was fashionable like Travis, but in a more casual, laid back sort of way. As Spike sat there, he listened to Travis' and Steve's conversation.

"I don't know, man, the last time I saw Bart was at the football game two days ago," Steve said as Travis sipped his coffee. "It's not like Bart to miss classes or a practice session with the coach on the field. I hope he's okay.

"Yeah, me too. The last time I saw him was in the locker room after the game," Bart said. "He seemed to be okay. I mean he was already wearing his navy blue silk socks and matching boxer briefs. He was ready to get all suited up and hang out here. He had asked me to join you guys, but I had, uh, another engagement."

"Yeah, I know, I got here with our suit buddy Scott J. that day and when you didn't show up we figured you were just too exhausted from the game. But when Bart didn't show up either, well, we knew that he was exhausted as well, but it was him who had suggested we all come here," Steve said, crossing a leg over his knee. "So I really hope he's okay."

"I checked with his professors and they said he wasn't in class yesterday or today," Travis added. "I called his dorm room phone number, but there was no answer, and I even called—"

Travis' words were cut short when he heard Spike's boots landing on the tabletop behind them. Spike had heard enough about Travis' buddy, Bart, he'd had enough of seeing the guy sitting there sipping coffee and eating snacks with his golden haired buddy. The skinhead wanted his jock pussy and he wanted him now!

"What the hell was that?" Steve asked.

He and Travis both turned to see Spike at the table nearby.

Travis gulped hard, but kept silent as Spike lit a cigarette with the gold lighter that Travis had given him, then smirked at the two suited buddies and stood up. He sauntered out of the food court blowing smoke down at Travis as he passed by his and Steve's table.

"Holy fuck, that lowlife skin just tainted you with his cancerous smoke," Steve said, half rising from his chair. "I say we go and make short work of that asshole."

"No!" Travis shouted, but quickly collected himself and glanced over at Spike, who was looking over his shoulder.

He subtly gestured for Travis to follow him.

"No? What do you mean, no???" Steve asked as Travis placed a hand on his shoulder and moved him back into his chair. "The guy is a lowlife skin; he blew smoke on you, what the hell, man?"

"It, uh, it was no big deal, Steve," Travis said. "Look, I have to meet with a professor of mine, I just remembered, I have to go."

With that, Travis gulped down what was left of his coffee, dropped a few bills on the table in front of Steve, asked him to pay for his share of their meal and then told him he would see him later.

"Yeah, uh, sure, I guess," Steve said. "And listen, if you hear from Bart, let me know, huh?"

"Sure thing, bud," Travis called out over his shoulder as he headed out of the food court.

When he stepped out of the food court, Travis spied Spike heading out the main entrance of the mall. He quickly followed after him, his wingtip heels clicking on the sparkling clean floor of the mall as he trotted along. Travis seemed to be almost in a trance of sorts, hypnotized by the fact that his skin had beckoned him to follow, and Travis knew only too well where the skin would want him to follow him to, the back alley of the Cherry Hill mall, namely, the trash alley.

When Travis made his way out of the main entrance of the mall, he quickly sauntered over to the trash alley, and sure enough, there was Spike, standing by the oversized dumpster, two huge shopping bags from Neiman Marcus placed atop the dumpster. Travis took in the sight of Spike standing there smoking his cigarette, a smug expression on his face. Spike was wearing his ever-present trademark worn jeans with oil and dirt stains on them, a wife beater tee that had seen better days, and his trademark black construction boots, them all scuffed, grimy and dirty. As Travis approached, he quickly slowed down his pace and lowered his head so that he was looking directly at Spike's boots as he neared him.

"Good to see you, jock pussy," Spike said meanly as Travis snapped to attention, yet kept his head lowered so he stared only at the skin's boots.

Travis nodded, acknowledging Spike's greeting.

"Got you trained so well, huh jock pussy?" Spike said and Travis nodded. "You know better than to speak until I tell you to."

Once more Travis nodded and was relieved when Spike barked, "Permission to speak, jock pussy."

Travis looked up, smiled a bit and then said, "Sir, what are those two bags on the dumpster?"

"Your stuff, all your stuff," Spike replied, then reached out and grabbed the knot in Travis' tie and pulled him close.

He again blew smoke in Travis' face, but Travis made no objection, instead he smiled wider as Spike held him by the tie.

"And the tapes?" Travis said, his coffee breath invading Spike's nostrils and mouth.

Spike savored the scent of his jock pussy as he hauled him closer by the knot in his tie. Everything about him was beautiful to the skin, up to and including the scent of coffee on his breath.

"Destroyed, totally gone, jock pussy, but they weren't tapes, they were actually DVDs," Spike replied, and without thinking, Travis yanked the cigarette from between Spike's lips, threw it to the ground, wrapped his football player sized arms around Spike and clamped his mouth down on the skinhead's.

Spike grunted as Travis kissed him, not once taking his lips off the skin's.

Spike responded by reaching around Travis, cupping his ass cheeks in his big, grimy hands, gripping them hard and hoisting his angel, his jock pussy, a few inches off the ground. Travis kissed his skin harder yet, his cock stiff and fully erect to its full nine inches in his suit pants.

"Thank you, Sir, thank you," Travis moaned and before Spike could respond, he slammed his lips down on his again.

Spike grunted a second time as Travis' coffee tasting tongue explored his cigarette tasting mouth.

Spike gripped Travis' ass cheeks tighter, inflicting some erotic pain, lifted him a tad higher off the concrete and tipped him over toward him, kissing him harder as well.

Travis stopped kissing Spike after another short while and looked down at the man he now thought of as his savior.

"I know you'll probably punish me for this display of affection, Sir, but you have no idea how thankful I am at this moment," Travis said as Spike hefted him a tad higher.

The handsome college student leaned down and kissed the skin's bald head a few times.

"I'll allow it, for the moment, jock pussy," Spike said as he looked at Travis' smiling face.

"So, how did you manage to get the DVDs away from John?" Travis asked, his hands now behind Spike's neck.

"Let's just say I can be very persuasive when I need to be, jock pussy," Spike said and then kissed Travis once more on the mouth and slowly set him back down on the ground. "I got to say, boy, I love hoistin' you like that, but you're no goddamned lightweight. You can check the bags now to make sure everything is there."

As Travis did just that, Spike said, "And you won't have to worry about that fucker, John Broderick, harassing you anymore, jock pussy. He knows what the fuck I'll do to him if he as much as looks at you the wrong way."

"Th—thank you, Sir, I honestly don't know what to say or do," Travis began but Spike held up a hand, stopping the college boy in mid-sentence.

"Oh, I think you know what to do, jock pussy. You know very well what the fuck to do, now get busy doing it!!!" Spike ordered.

Shaking a bit from Spike's outburst, but not feeling half the fear he usually felt when in the skin's presence, Travis made his way slowly to his knees in front of the man who had so enslaved him.

On his knees, Travis leaned down further till his face was closer than close to Spike's black work boots. Without having to be told to do so, Travis stuck out his tongue and began licking and lapping feverishly at Spike's boots. He spit on them a few times and licked up his spit, swallowing it along with all the grime that was on Spike's boots.

"Fucking trained you just right, jock pussy," Spike said gleefully.

"Thank you, Sir," Travis responded without looking up.

Spike watched as Travis then moved to his other boot and spit on it a few times, licked it and kissed it and swallowed the grime and spit that was on it.

Spike reached down and gently trailed the front of one hand over the top of Travis's soft hair, caressing it.

Travis looked up for a moment and saw the adoration for him in Spike's eyes.

"Sir, thank you, Sir," Travis whispered and Spike saw the same look of adoration in Travis' eyes as well.

"Alright, enough with this lovey shmoozey stuff," Spike said, then lifted one booted foot and pressed it meanly against Travis' white shirt and pushed hard on his chest.

Travis fell back, landing on his muscular back, his feet pressed against the ground.

"Collect your stuff and let's go to your dorm room so you can change out of that fancy suit of yours. You and I are taking a ride in my pickup truck." Spike said with total authority.

As Spike sauntered past Travis, the college jock quickly got to his feet, glanced down at the footprint that Spike's boot had made on his pristine white shirt, grabbed his two bags that Spike had retrieved from John, and dashed after the skin.

"But Sir, where are we—"

Spike looked at jock pussy, rage now showing in the skin's eyes. All jock pussy could so was stop. He had spoken without permission. Instantly, he apologized, then stood at attention, ready to feel the back of Spike's hand against his cheek. But Spike did not slap him this time. Instead, Spike asked, "You got any classes this afternoon, jock pussy?"

Travis remained at attention and shook his head.

"Then, like I said, we're going for a ride in my pickup," Spike said, then stepped next to Travis and grabbed the collars of his suit jacket.

Travis gasped as his tie knot pressed against his Adam's apple.

"And as for where we're going, let's just say you need *more* training."

With that, Spike and Travis walked out of the trash alley, with Spike holding tight to Travis' collar, oblivious to what any passerby would think at the sight of them.

When they reached the parking lot of the Cherry Hill Mall, Spike walked Travis over to his pickup truck.

"Got your car here somewhere, jock pussy?" Spike asked. "Nod your response to me, no more talking for you."

Travis nodded.

"You'll get it when we get back from where we're going," Spike said as he walked Travis by his collar to the back of the truck, where he had a lot of grungy tool boxes, spare tires, carjacks, and other items normally found in the back section of a guy's pickup truck. "You'll ride back here. Toss those bags in, jock pussy."

Travis did as he was told and looked questioningly at the skin.

"Oh yes, you're riding in there, jock pussy, and I don't want to hear no back talk or flack about it," Spike said, then quickly scooped Travis up off the ground, then into his arms for a moment, then tossed the handsome jock into the back section of the pickup truck.

Spike got into the front seat, and in seconds Travis' suit was all mussed up and he was being careened and jostled all over the place as Spike drove toward the Calderfield College like a bat out of hell while smoking a cigarette. Travis heard him thundering the words, "Fucking jock pussy, you made me love you, you silk socked guy!!"

When they reached the Calderfield College campus, Spike pulled up in front of Travis' dorm and climbed out of the pickup. He sauntered over to the back of the truck and took in the sight of the mussed up, dusty Travis, his classy looking suit in much need of a good dry cleaning. Spike hawed a few times at the sight of his boot print on Travis' white shirt. As he sat up amid all the mess in the back of the pickup, Travis grabbed his two shopping bags and looked once more at the man he had come to call his Sir, his Master.

"Climb the fuck out of there, go to your room and change into a pair of Spandex shorts, a tee shirt, sneakers and sweat socks," Spike said.

Without a word of protest, Travis did as he was told.

"And be back here as quickly as possible, no wasting time, jock pussy," Spike ordered as Travis climbed out of the back section of the pickup.

A few students heading to and from classes saw the strange spectacle of Travis being ordered around by the skin, but simply minded their business and continued on their way. To them, Travis was the hero of the recent football game, and if he wanted to hang out with a scummy and smelly looking pierced and tattooed skinhead, well, they figured that was the handsome jock's business. As long as he continued to win football games for their prestigious college, most of the students felt that Travis could do no wrong and could do whatever the fuck he wanted.

As Travis trudged toward his dorm room, he tried to wipe some of the dust and grime off his classy dark suit.

"Damn, why do I get myself all dressed up when I know he's going to make a mess of me?" Travis asked himself and a few minutes later, he was in his room.

He did not see Chad Towers there, figuring the guy had classes that afternoon. Travis quickly stored the two shopping bags in a closet and stripped out of his suit, all the while wondering what in all hell Spike could have in mind for him now.

Within ten minutes, Travis was redressed in a pair of black Spandex knee-length shorts, a white muscle shirt, which showed off his well-formed biceps and triceps to great advantage, and white ankle length sweat socks by Nike and a pair of black and white sneakers by New Balance. Quickly checking his look in a full-length mirror, Travis figured that Spike would approve. He grabbed a fanny pack, stored his wallet and keys in it and dashed out of his dorm room. Travis trotted across the campus to where Spike was waiting.

"Sure as fuck took you long enough," Spike railed as Travis approached.

"P—permission to speak, Sir?" Travis asked nervously once he was standing in front of Spike.

Spike looked jock pussy over. "Sure, for now, what's on your mind, jock pussy?"

"Well, Sir, I got changed as quickly as possible, so I'm sorry if you were waiting all that long, Sir," Travis quibbled.

At that moment, Spike was glad he had granted his jock pussy boy permission to speak.

"Also Sir, I'm just wondering where we're going and—"

"You'll find out when we get there," Spike replied. "Now let's be on our way, huh?"

"Sir. Yes, Sir," Travis responded and went to climb into the back section of the pickup truck.

"No, you're riding in the passenger seat this time," Spike said as he pulled the keys from his jeans pocket.

"Sir?" Travis asked as he headed toward the passenger side door.

"Where I'm taking you, you need to be all clean and proper, if you ride back there again, you'll get all mussed up and dusty all over again, and I can't have that," Spike explained as he climbed into the driver's seat and jock pussy got settled on the passenger side. They stole a glance at each other, each thankful to have found each other.

Spike turned the key in the ignition, then said to Travis, "Seatbelt yourself in, jock pussy." He drove off, taking his precious cargo with him.

"Settle back and relax, we have a long drive ahead of us," Spike said as he pulled out into traffic. "At least an hour or more."

"Y—yes Sir," Travis replied and saw Spike placing a cigarette between his lips.

Travis quickly reached into his fanny pack, pulled out the gold lighter and lit the skin's cigarette.

"Good boy," Spike said, and then blew smoke in jock pussy's direction.

Then, not wanting to take advantage of the fact that Spike had granted him permission to speak, jock pussy simply settled back in the passenger seat and stared straight ahead.

While Travis was being driven to an unknown destination, his football buddy, Bart Findley, was waking up in the trash alley of the Cherry Hill Mall.

"Awww, fuck, wh—whaaaaa happened?" Bart grumbled as he came to, propped up atop a closed, oversized garbage can, his back against the concrete wall. "Fucking steam must've knocked me out and—"

Bart's thoughts were cut short when he felt the sucking sensations at his nipples, a few of his toes, and sore, over-spent cock.

The football god's eyes shot open and his vision cleared and adjusted to the hazy sunlight. He was naked and in the trash alley of the Cherry Hill Mall, propped up on a giant garbage can, and being feasted on by four grimy, stinking homeless men.

As Bart looked downward, he saw a black homeless man, dressed in jeans a few sizes big for him, two different shoes on his feet, and a grimy white tank top sucking at his two big toes as he held the football player's naked feet tightly together. Bart's navy blue sheer socks were gone, along with his garters. At his nipples, two white homeless men, both of them wearing tan overcoats that looked like they had been found in the garbage along with tattered jeans and one of them in old, torn up sneakers and the other in oversized shoes, stood on either side of the beefy jock, bent down, their mangy mouths working at sucking and slurping and outright nursing savagely on Bart's big, man-sized tits. And lastly, but most unbelievably, there was a toothless homeless man who appeared to be a mix between white and black and to be at least in his late seventies, bent over the side of one of the men sucking at Bart's nipples, busily sucking and slurping on Bart's overused cock, Bart's balls cupped in his hand as he sucked away.

"Oh God, what is this?" Bart screamed as his head cleared. "FUCK, I can't seem to stop bein' used like a goddamned buffet."

The sounds of slurping filled the area and Bart pressed the back of his head against the concrete wall, grimacing in a mixture of forced ecstasy and outright rage.

Realizing that his hands were still tied behind him as the four homeless men were feasting on him, Bart looked around and whimpered, "How the fucks did I get here?"

The guy at Bart's feet looked up at him, grinned through a mouthful of missing teeth and said, "Two of my homeboys carried you in here and plopped you down on the pail you is presently on, you bound god," and then he pressed Bart's big feet back together and resumed sucking the football player's big toes.

Bart moaned again.

"Yeah, and when they left you on the garbage pail like so much trash, they each took one of the pretty silk socks you was wearing," one of the guys munching on Bart's nipples said, his breath dank and rancid as he spoke.

"Said they wanted those socks of yours as a souvenir."

The homeless man resumed sucking Bart's nipple and Bart cried out, "Fucking souvenir of the fact that they snagged my sexy ass out of the Calderfield College locker room after our momentous football game the other day, oh God, take it easy with me, dudes."

"Fucking skins used me like a fucked up sex machine," Bart grumbled and glanced around himself in utter disbelief. "And now, look at this, now I got four homeless dudes feasting the fuck out of me."

The toothless man who was sucking Bart's sore cock looked up at the handsome jock for a moment and Bart saw that his garters were dangling around the man's neck.

"Yeah, our skin-headed homeboys told us you were one fucking dee-lite," the toothless man said.

Bart looked sorrowfully at the man's toothless mouth.

"Now you just relax, football boy, I gots here the best mouth on the planet to be suckin' cock with—"

"Oh, my poor cock," Bart railed as the man sucked his cock back into his gummy mouth.

It drove Bart nearly insane with twisted pleasure as he felt the toothless man's tongue, lips and gums scrounging all over his hard cock.

A short while later Bart shot a dry load into the homeless man's mouth and the man drove the football player nearly over the edge as he continued sucking his overly sensitized cock. Actually, he sucked Bart until he pissed strong and hard. The toothless man drank that down as well.

Once Bart was done pissing, the four men all switched the areas they were presently sucking on and went to town on the poor trussed up guy again.

Bart railed as his tits, toes and cock were sucked again and again.

"Least you dudes can do for me when you're done is find me some clothes to wear and untie my hands." Bart sniveled as the four men treated him like a buffet table at a wedding.

The man sucking Bart's cock squeezed the jock's balls and Bart felt his nuts begin cooking up another dry load, to be stolen by the homeless guy.

"Fuck!!!" Bart cried out.

The four homeless men snickered around the areas of Bart that they were presently feasting on.

While Bart was suffering through his latest sexual tribulations, Spike had stopped his pickup along a lonely road to get out and stretch his legs a bit. He ordered jock pussy to do the same, handing the jock a bottle of cool mineral water from a cooler he had had stored in the back of the truck.

As the men stood by the truck sipping water, jock pussy said, "Thank you for the water, Sir."

"No problem, jock pussy," Spike replied.

"It, uh, looks like the ride is taking longer than you indicated," jock pussy said, looking around the desolate area. "You had said it would take an hour or so."

"I'm takin' the scenic route," Spike replied sarcastically and spit a mouthful of water in Travis' face.

"Wh—what was that for, Sir???" jock pussy quibbled miserably, quickly wiping his face with the back of his hand.

"I gave you permission to speak, jock pussy, and it wasn't so you could state the obvious. I expect better statements and quotes from someone of your stature," Spike railed at jock pussy and spit more water in his face. "You think I don't know that it's takin' us longer than I said to get to Leo's Estate, jock pussy?"

At the sound of "Leo's Estate," jock pussy's heart skipped a beat. He pulled the bottle of water away from his lips and looked at Spike in disbelief.

"Th—that's where you're taking me, Sir???" jock pussy asked, his heart thundering in fear.

"Yeah jock pussy, it's the perfect place for the training *you need,*" Spike replied and snapped his fingers.

At the sound of Spike's fingers snapping, jock pussy stood instantly at attention.

"And when we get there, I expect you to do me right by behaving accordingly, is that clear?" Spike railed in jock pussy's face.

"Sir, yes Sir," jock pussy replied because he had to. "But do I really need training, Sir???"

"You speak when you don't have my permission, you lack self-confidence in important areas of your life, you disobey me without even realizing it, you need me to constantly remind you of things," Spike railed at jock pussy, who was sweating in the hot sun. Spike grabbed the bottle of water from him and poured it over jock pussy's head. Travis did not move from his stance of attention.

"So, *yes*, YOU do need the kind of training that Leo's Estate offers, jock pussy," Spike concluded. "Now, let's get a move-on, huh."

Once the two men were seated back in the pickup truck, jock pussy's mind wandered a bit as Spike drove. Over the years, the handsome jock had heard of Leo's Estate. He whispered the words, *"Galley Slave Training?"* and stared straight ahead.

From what Travis knew of Leo's Estate, it was a huge manor house built in the country just after the Civil War. The man who created it was named Leo Shatterhand and was himself a war profiteer, hence the reason it came to be called Leo's Estate. The manor proper was used as a headquarters for masters and their chambers, while the *equipment* was held in the outbuildings and in certain circumstances, the subs. Because the organization of Leo's Estate helped found The Estate, it was run by a board of wealthy directors, and managed to stay afloat despite world wars and economic downturns.

The Estate was a a Shingle Style building that had been popular after the North American Civil War. The Estate had prospered throughout the years thanks to many people in need of the kind of training for which jock pussy was being brought.

As time went on, offshoots of Leo's Estate began to crop up everywhere, including one branch that was situated in the country area a few hours' drive from Calderfield College. Travis knew that this particular branch of Leo's Estate catered to the training of Galley Slaves, or, most notably, Rowing. But it was not just any ordinary kind of rowing, it was outright sadistic rowing that trainees were brought for.

* * *

As Spike drove, he glanced over at Travis a few times, noticing that his angelic college boy was turning more and more pale.

Spike grinned meanly and pressed his foot to the accelerator.

It was more than two hours later since they had started out when Spike and Travis arrived at the front gates of the mammoth looking manor. Spike stopped his pickup truck in front of the closed gates, and a few moments later a guard in a gray uniform with well-shined knee high boots approached the truck. He was nearly six feet tall, with blond hair under his uniform cap. He had a boyish face and it appeared to Travis that the guard was just about bursting out of his uniform due to his oversized, muscular body. At the sight of the boyishly handsome gate guard, Travis' cock stirred a bit in his Spandex shorts.

"May I help you, Sir?" the guard asked Spike, leaning down next to the driver's side window.

"Yeah, tell Coach Wilkinson that Lloyd, a.k.a. Spike, is here with his latest trainee." Spike replied.

The guard and Spike each glanced over at a very terror-stricken looking Travis.

"I'll be glad to, Sir," the guard said and licked his lips.

Spike and jock pussy watched as the guard stepped over to a telephone box, opened it with a key and dialed two digits.

"H—how," jock pussy began.

"How do I know about this place, jock pussy?" Spike asked.

Jock pussy simply nodded.

"Well, let's say that just because I didn't go to college like you're doing that I don't know of these things. In the world that I live in, Leo's Estate and places like it are pretty well known."

That said, Spike produced a cigarette and placed it between his lips. With his hands and fingers trembling, jock pussy reached over and lit the cigarette for him. Spike grinned meanly around the cigarette and blew smoke in jock pussy's direction.

"Fuckin' jock pussy," he muttered and then he and Travis saw the guard making his way back to the pickup truck.

"Sir, Coach Wilkinson said to cuff and blindfold your trainee and to bring him to his office," the guard said to Spike, then moved to open the main gates of Leo's Estate.

"Will do," Spike said. Once the gates were open, he drove on.

"S—Sir?" jock pussy whimpered. "C—cuff and blindfold me, Sir?"

"Relax, jock pussy, all of this is going to be for your own good," Spike said and flung his half smoked cigarette out the window. "Open the glove compartment."

Jock pussy did as he was told, and to his dismay, a pair of steel handcuffs dropped out. Jock pussy caught them and held them up.

"The key is in there as well, but you won't need it, jock pussy boy," Spike said and grabbed the cuffs from Travis.

A short while later, Spike parked his pickup truck in the area of a parking lot marked Guests. He and jock pussy stepped out of the vehicle, jock pussy having a tad bit of trouble stepping out, seeing as his hands were now locked behind him and Spike had tied a black bandanna over the jock's eyes. Once jock pussy was out of the truck, Spike took him by his upper arm and walked him to the main building of Leo's Estate.

What in all fucks am I doing here??? jock pussy thought. And why have I allowed this guy to take me in such a manner?

As they walked toward the main building of Leo's Estate, Spike saw other trainees in the clutches of their trainers, or more appropriately, in the clutches of their Masters.

Some of them were bound and gagged, others were dangling from their wrists from tree branches and being flogged, and some of them were out on boats in the lake and rowing, which was the main reason that Spike had brought his boy to The Estate.

As they walked along, Spike guiding his blindfolded charge, he now understood why all new trainees were brought to the main office in darkness, they were not to see some of the tribulations that they would be enduring during their hours or days at The Estate. As Spike walked with jock pussy, a muscular black man in the uniform of The Estate was guiding a blindfolded white guy out toward the lake. The white guy was wearing nothing but a pair of weightlifter's posing trunks and was built like a Greek god. Spike smiled meanly at the black guard as he and jock pussy passed him.

Once in the mansion-like building, Spike brought jock pussy to the office of the university rowing coach on the main floor, Alex Wilkinson, known to his contemporaries as Wilk, Coach, or Coach Wilk.

Spike knocked on the door until he heard, "Enter."

Spike opened the door and stepped inside, hauling jock pussy with him. "Hmm, that sure as hell ain't Coach Wilkinson."

"Good afternoon," a six foot two, approximately one hundred and ninety pound muscular guy with a forty four inch chest, a thirty one inch waist, a huge neck, iron-like calves, and huge biceps in a white tee shirt with the Leo's Estate university logo stitched onto the left side of it, along with black jeans and barefoot said.

"Sir, what is this???" jock pussy asked, taking in the sound of the maniacal muscle bound god's raspy voice.

Ignoring jock pussy's whining, Spike took in the sight of the man before them and said, "Well, Zeb, good to see you again, bud. It looks like Coach Wilk's training has worked wonders on you."

"Sure as fuck, Spike," Zeb said, then approached the skin and the two men shook hands roughly and vigorously. "Because now I'm a full-fledged trainer, and it looks like I get to train this sweet thing you got here."

At the sound of those words, jock pussy grimaced behind his blindfold.

"Where is Coach Wilk? He told the guard at the front gate for me to bring my trainee to his office," Spike said, holding tight to jock pussy's upper arm.

"He had to step out, but not to worry, my man, *I'm* here to take charge," Zeb said, grinning meanly. "Now, tell me what you'd like done with this sweet thing you got here."

Spike removed jock pussy's blindfold so Zeb could get the entire picture of him, and at the sight of Zeb, jock pussy's heart sunk like the Titanic. The college boy was terror-stricken.

But on the other hand, Zeb was gleefully and sadistically delighted at the sight of jock pussy's angelic face, and the rest of him as well.

"What I want done with *my* boy here is the same kind of training you yourself received, bud," Spike said.

"Th—the same kind of training he got???" jock pussy blurted in a mixture of anger and trepidation. "But Sir—"

"Well, you know the rules, Spike," Zeb replied, ignoring jock pussy's sniveling outburst. "Only members may order such training, and *you* will need to decide if this sweet thing here is a member or not."

Spike chuckled meanly, clutching jock pussy's arm tighter to show Zeb his ownership of the jock. Then Spike flipped Zeb the bird, which Zeb ignored.

Zeb said, "Okay, bud, dry land or on the water?"

"Sir, please, don't hand me over to this guy," jock pussy began, but Spikeignored him.

"On the water," Spike said. "This football diva needs to learn a lot more about teamwork. He's great on the football field at Calderfield College, but when it comes to my rules and regulations, well, he needs just a bit more of a kick in the ass."

"Calderfield College, eh, sweet thing?" Zeb asked jock pussy as he reached forward and tweaked one of jock pussy's nipples. He twisted it, getting a good loud yelp of pain out of the college boy. "Pretty fancy schmancy boy you are, huh?"

"Yeah, his daddy owns most of the town," Spike added. "But if his daddy could see him now, huh, jock pussy?"

"Jock pussy, huh?" Zeb asked Spike. "Is that what he's called?"

"It's what he is, so it's what I call him," Spike said as jock pussy looked woefully at him.

"Alright, seeing as Coach Wilk is a bit, uh, indisposed, I'll take charge here, Spike. You know you can count on me," Zeb said, looking hungrily at jock pussy. "I like that this sweet thing of yours is a football diva, as you so aptly called him. Personally, I feel that these college football dudes need a lot more coaching than what they get in their training on campus, so I can honestly say you've brought me some good fortune today, bud. Come on, let's go to my car."

Still barefoot, Zeb led the way out of Coach Wilkinson's office to a luxurious garage where a late model dark blue luxury Sedan was waiting.

"Seeing as you got the sweet thing there cuffed, Spike, stripping him will be difficult," Zeb said as he led the way.

"Stripping me?" jock pussy reeled.

"Not a problem at all, Zeb," Spike replied snidely and produced his ever-trusty switchblade. "This will be a pleasure."

As Spike proceeded to slice and cut off jock pussy's athletic clothing, Zeb sighed and opened the trunk of the Sedan.

"Sir, please, my clothes, you-you made me put all this on," jock pussy begged, but his words fell on deaf ears.

At the sight of the open car trunk, tears filled the handsome jock's eyes.

When jock pussy was naked except for his sneakers and short white sweat socks, he cried miserably. Then Spike took his face in his hands and told him he was leaving him in Zeb's care.

"Sir please, no, no," jock pussy whined. "Please, at least come with me to wherever he's going to be taking me, please, Sir."

As the tears streamed down jock pussy's face, Spike's heart thundered in his chest. He could not believe that this incredibly beautiful, muscular, college boy was his and would be for the rest of his life. Spike smiled meanly, leaned in and kissed jock pussy hard on the mouth; kissed his face, and even licked some of the college boy's tears off his face.

"You fucking do what Zeb tells you, no more backtalk, jock pussy," Spike said. "All of this is for your own good. You actually brought yourself here, you know that!!"

Then Spike scooped jock pussy up off the ground, into his hugely muscular arms and forced him into the trunk of Zeb's car. Looking up at Spike, jock pussy watched in fear as the trunk lid was slammed shut.

Sniveling miserably, jock pussy balled his cuffed hands into one big fist, clenched his teeth, and from within the trunk, heard Zeb get in the front seat, then Spike telling Zeb to take good care of his special boy, and then the car pulled out.

A while later, jock pussy had no sense of just how long he had been in the trunk, his only company back there being a carjack and a spare tire. Now that his Spandex shorts and muscle tee shirt had been cut and shredded, jock pussy wondered what he would wear for his training with Zeb *and* more importantly, what he would be wearing when Spike brought him back to the college campus. He had all too many memories of the last outfit Spike had supplied him with for a ride back to his campus.

As the car plowed along, jock pussy lost even more sense of time. He sweated in fear, wondered where in all hell he was being taken and wondered just how intense Galley Slave Training would be. It was what Leo's Estate was known for, after all. Jock pussy also wondered why Leo's Estate would have Spike as a member. Who was Spike *really,* after all?

All jock pussy knew of Spike was that he was a raunchy, filthy, sweaty smelling, pierced and tattooed street thug who wore worn jeans, sweat stained wife beater's and the dirtiest scuffed up construction boots he had ever seen. At the thought of Spike's boots, jock pussy's cock began to engorge to its full nine throbbing inches. Yes, jock pussy wondered who the hell Spike really was. All he knew of him thus far was that the mangy guy had managed to seduce and literally enslave him via his work boots, and that his name was Lloyd.

After what seemed like an eternity, the car stopped long enough for jock pussy to wonder if the trip was over or if perhaps Zeb had stopped to stretch his legs. If that were the case, jock pussy hoped that Zeb would let him out of the trunk long enough to stretch his legs as well.

Jock pussy heard the driver's side door open and then slam shut, and then the sound of boots crunching on gravel as Zeb approached the back of the car. The trunk was opened and flooded with sunlight. As jock pussy squinted to allow his eyes to readjust to the light, Zeb ordered him out. Struggling awkwardly, jock pussy swung his muscular legs over the rim of the trunk and Zeb quickly relieved him of the last of his clothing, yanking his sneakers and sweat socks off jock pussy's feet and dumping them in the trunk.

"You won't need any footwear where you're going, sweet thing," Zeb said and then hauled jock pussy the rest of the way out of the trunk.

Once jock pussy was standing, totally naked, outside the car, Zeb slammed the trunk closed.

Jock pussy took in the sight of Zeb, who was also naked but for a leather harness and a series of leather straps from his huge neck to his crotch; no hair below the neck. He was branded with a tattoo of numbers on his left pectoral and his cock was in a metal sort of tube device, one end of which was attached to the harness, the other end attached to an ampallang.*

As jock pussy looked Zeb over, his own cock betrayed him as it stuck out long and hard. Jock pussy did not recall the car stopping long enough for Zeb to have changed into the attire he was presently wearing. He figured he must have been disoriented in the trunk of the car during the ride, or he had slept or blacked out during some of it.

As jock pussy continued taking in Zeb, he realized that the man had only his right testicle. Not knowing what to say at the moment, jock pussy simply looked around and saw that they were in a parking lot surrounded by a forest.

Jock pussy was suddenly distracted when he saw two naked pony slaves being hitched to a cart by a pony mistress and in the cart was his football coach from Calderfield College.

If Zeb noticed the look of shock in jock pussy's eyes at the sight of his macho football coach being made into a pony slave, he gave no indication of it whatsoever. Instead, he tweaked one of jock pussy's delectable nipples and asked him if he was used to walking or running barefoot.

Jock pussy looked at Zeb most miserably and muttered, "No."

In response, Zeb smiled fiendishly and said, "Well, in that case, walk slowly and carefully, sweet thing."

"Wh—what is this place?" jock pussy asked as he hunched his broad shoulders up in supplication.

As they walked side by side, Zeb explained that it was a private part of Leo's Estate used to train slaves. Grabbing jock pussy's upper arm in a tight grip, Zeb said, "You needn't worry, sweet thing, there's hundreds of acres here, and we have total privacy, so there's no chance of anyone capturing a video of you."

Zeb laughed meanly at the irony of his joke, squeezed jock pussy's arm tighter yet, and the two men walked on.

As they walked in silence for the next few minutes, jock pussy saw a basic training unit of muscular men, all naked, run by them. Actually, only the recruits were naked but for boots and backpacks, the trainers leading the group were fully clothed in army fatigues.

"Why me, Zeb? Why was I brought here?" jock pussy asked.

"It's what your Master wants, sweet thing, and what your Master wants, he gets," Zeb replied.

"But I don't have a Master," jock pussy said.

"Whatever you choose to call him then, whether it be Dom, Top, Sir, Coach, whatever you call Spike, however you see him, he is your Master, sweet thing," Zeb said, and as he spoke, jock pussy's cock engorged some more and dribbled pre-cum. "So, if you don't have something permanent that you call him—"

"I—I call him Sir, he is my boot Sir, I suppose you could say," jock pussy explained. "What do you call Spike?"

Zeb laughed and said, I call Spike a member in bad standing. I know enough about him to have him expelled from his membership, but Spike knows too much about our organization here to do that, so it's a catch twenty-two, you might say, sweet thing."

"So I'm his slave, I'm Spike's slave, his boy," jock pussy said, his head hanging down and looking at his hard cock as he said it. "Is that how things are going to be for me from now on, Zeb?"

"Looks to me like that's how you both want it, sweet thing," Zeb said. "Seeing as Spike brought you here for training and seeing as you didn't kick his ass yet, God knows you're built big enough to break him in two. Yes, it looks to me like you both want it this way. But it seems like you're still wrestling with some part of yourself over it all, and that's for you to figure out. My job is to train you as Spike has requested. Now, Leo's Estate is mostly used for basic or pony training. But there's also a large lake where we're headed now that's used for training galley slaves. That's what you're here for, sweet thing."

"But, I don't row," jock pussy said.

Zeb chuckled and said, "You do now, sweet thing. You see, you're going to be trained today as a galley slave whether you want to be or not."

"Is that what you are, Zeb, a galley slave, or are you Coach Wilkinson's boy? How do you define yourself?" jock pussy asked.

"I call myself Coach Wilkinson's protégé," Zeb replied. "But as for you, maybe you want to be known as Spike's sub, his boy, his bottom; those are all the terms that define you, sweet thing. Or did you mean what am I called here at Leo's Estate? If that's what you meant, then I'm simply known as Zeb, or Mrs. Wilk."

Jock pussy grinned, glanced to the side at the monster-sized guy and said, "I find that hard to believe, Zeb."

"Then I suggest during your time here that you talk to some of the femme doms," Zeb said. "You see, as a slave, or more appropriately as Coach Wilkinson's Mrs., I clean house; I cook, seeing as I am a trained gourmet chef; I fix things, I'm a real handy man; and I also organize practice time for our crew here at Leo's Estate. So you can see, sweet thing, I am pretty well-rounded. And if I am good, Coach Wilkinson lets me suck off some of our students. If I'm not good, I receive corporal punishment. Our relationship has lasted longer because of those things, and to be honest, what me and the coach share *is* more like a marriage."

"How uh, how long have you and the coach been married?" jock pussy asked.

"Well, let's just say that I've been the coach's property for seventeen years, sweet thing. Half of my life, actually," Zeb replied. "And that's why I'm branded with Coach Wilkinson's monogram and tattooed with an inventory number."

For a moment Zeb let go of jock pussy's arm, stepped in front of him and turned around. On his well-formed and exposed butt cheeks, jock pussy saw that Zeb was branded with a phallic monogram on one cheek and the number 013 on the other butt cheek.

"Fuck, what a piece of ass," jock pussy mused to himself and then saw the lake.

"And here we are," Zeb said, turning back to face jock pussy. "That's the Leviathan, by the way, sweet thing."

The Leviathan was a large boat with a huge platform. There were eight stations set up on its opposite sides and eight naked, bound muscular men on the left side, seven were on the right side. Jock pussy saw the space that was still open, waiting to be occupied. No doubt he would be occupying that space, he knew. In the middle of the platform, jock pussy saw a large raised chair facing in the opposite direction of the rowers. Behind the chair, facing the other direction, was a giant drum on its side.

"And there is Coach Wilkinson," Zeb said, pointing at the Leviathan.

Jock pussy took in the sight of the mighty Coach Wilkinson on the chair. He was handsome, looked to be in his early sixties and dressed in trousers and a windcheater along with a poplin rain hat and topsiders. Two other men, dressed more conventionally as tops, were checking the rowers and their oars.

As they got closer, jock pussy saw that the rowers were bound to the sliding seats, stretchers, pommels.

Seconds later, Zeb and jock pussy were boarding the boat.

Zeb let go of jock pussy's arm and walked ahead of him.

Jock pussy followed him to the empty seat.

Zeb meanly pushed jock pussy down onto the sliding seat and squatted beside him. Zeb squatted with his feet flat on the deck, his bottom in line with his ankles, his knees up, arms free to move. To jock pussy, the well-toned and overly muscular Zeb looked like an animal sitting on its haunches.

As for jock pussy, Zeb fastened his feet into stretchers and locked them in place. Chains between cuffs were wrapped around the pommels of the oar and both of jock pussy's hands were then manacled to the oar as well; and lastly, a shackle was locked around jock pussy's balls. Zeb wasn't all that gentle as he handled jock pussy's manhood.

As Zeb shackled jock pussy's nut sac, the college boy glanced at the trainer's lone testicle. Looking up and into jock pussy's eyes Zeb told him quietly, "That's not what happened, sweet thing, you're perfectly safe. Spike said to train you, not deform you."

As jock pussy was manacled in place, one of the two nearby leather men stepped behind the giant drum and hit it a few times with a drumstick. The other leather man took out a single tail whip and cracked it in midair, as much to warm up as to show it off.

Zeb then explained to jock pussy how to row. He told him to push with his legs, when his legs were extended, he was to pull with his arms as he leaned back, then push forward with his arms and roll forward on the wheels of the sliding seat.

"Then the pommel is turned so that the blade of the oar is either parallel to the surface of the water or perpendicular to it," Zeb went on, squatting next to jock pussy as he spoke. "On the stroke, the push back, the blade is in in the water and perpendicular; on the recovery, the blade is above the water and parallel."

Zeb ordered jock pussy to practice a few strokes, and then suddenly the whip master cracked the whip loudly. To jock pussy, it sounded like three gunshots.

With that Coach Wilkinson shouted, "Cast off!"

The drummer hit a slow beat, the rowers started to move the oars and the seats and the Leviathan left the pier.

Zeb counted one for the stroke and two for the recovery as jock pussy did his best to keep his rhythm and control steady. Jock pussy could sense that Zeb had stood up and stepped to Coach Wilkinson's chair. There, Zeb squatted onto his haunches again like some exotic pet. Feeling miserable, jock pussy turned away from the scene of Zeb and Coach Wilkinson and fleetingly wondered about his football coach from Calderfield College and how he was faring as a pony boy. But then, suddenly, jock pussy's thoughts were cut short as, instead of being guided by Zeb's counting and the drum's rhythm, jock pussy received the whip across his muscular back to keep him in place.

Jock pussy roared loudly in pain as the whip master lashed him twice more across the back.

"Keep your rhythm boy!!" Coach Wilkinson shouted over at jock pussy.

As jock pussy did his damndest to row properly, his biceps and triceps bulged and burned as he worked the oar back and forth. He glanced over and saw Zeb pointing at him and whispering in Coach

Wilkinson's ear.

The coach looked over at jock pussy and smiled from ear to ear and then clapped his hands a few times. Somehow jock pussy figured that Coach Wilkinson knew Spike and now knew that he was there because of Spike. When the whip master saw jock pussy looking over at Coach Wilkinson and Zeb, he again brought his whip down hard across his now sweating back. The sound of the whip cracking against his back was maddening to jock pussy; the feeling of it was like being stung by a thousand bees at the same time.

"Please, man!" jock pussy cried out miserably and fell back into a rhythmic rowing motion. "I didn't sign on for any of this."

Smiling wickedly, Coach Wilkinson whispered to Zeb, "It looks like the sweet thing, as you call him, will require thorough training." Zeb nodded, wallowing in watching jock pussy suffer as he was again whipped.

At the outset, the Leviathan made figure eights in the lake, first left, then right, over and over again, the oarsmen, including jock pussy, being whipped when necessary and sweating and grunting through the nearly backbreaking work as they rowed and rowed.

At Coach Wilkinson's command, the pace was changed to twenty-two strokes per minute and then thirty-two; and if an oarsman did not keep pace, he was savagely whipped. When the man whipping the oarsmen shouted out for a power ten, jock pussy quickly found out that a power ten is ten strokes at full strength as fast as the oarsmen were able to manage. Jock pussy also quickly learned that on turns, one side rows while the other side holds the oars up, blades parallel to the water.

Jock pussy fell into the rhythm of the rowing, not wanting to be whipped any more. He also realized that he was very sexually aroused, his cock had not deflated once while rowing or while being whipped, and he wondered about Zeb and Coach Wilkinson, not to mention his own football coach, who he had seen in the cart with the two ponies. Jock pussy recalled then how his football coach had trained him on the Calderfield College football field to pull heavy objects with a harness.

* * *

While jock pussy rowed and was whipped when sluggish, Bart Findley was still dealing with his own degradations in the trash alley of the Cherry Hill Mall. He was now alone with the mulatto and toothless homeless man, the other three homeless men having feasted enough on the footballer.

"C—c'mon, man, give a dude a break here, huh," Bart pleaded after the homeless man's three buddies scampered off and he was now helping Bart off the top of the filthy garbage can that Jerome and Darren had set him down on.

Bart, feeling miserable, overly sexually used and his entire muscular body feeling hyper- sensitive to the touch now found himself not only with his hands still bound behind him, making him totally powerless against the homeless guy who was miniscule compared to him, but now, blindfolded as well, with the last of his clothing that he had been wearing, specifically his elastic garters.

Bart felt himself being propped up against the concrete wall in the trash alley as the man guided him by holding him by one upper arm and by a handful of his low hanging very drained balls.

"Can't let you go just yet, Mr. dee-lite," the toothless man said, squeezing and wagging Bart's testicles in his fist. "I needs me some more new-trition, ha! It's not every day that a guy like me gets to eat from a guy like you."

"Aw, no, no, not again, man," Bart whimpered seconds later as he felt his cock being engulfed into the toothless man's smooth, soft mouth. When the man swirled his mangy tongue all over Bart's soft cock, the football player felt his tortured balls churning like a butter churn.

"Ah Gawd," Bart gasped as the man careened his cock tip against his gums. "What a feeling."

"Heh, heh, no one can resist my mouth," the toothless man said and quickly and greedily slurped Bart's now semi hardness back into his craw.

As the man sucked him up to a pain-filled new erection, Bart pressed the ropes binding his wrists against the wall behind him and began rubbing them hard.

"Got to get out of this," Bart said to himself. "By hook or by crook

I have to get out of this mess."

As the man sucked Bart's cock, squeezed his swollen balls with one hand and caressed his muscled rear end at the same time, Bart found himself swiveling sexily and stupidly on his bare toes, dancing to the rhythm that the homeless man was forcing on him.

Bart panted, drenched in sweat, as he felt like he was being taken to the point of no return.

"Feels like my cock is tingling in your mouth, man," Bart grunted.

As the man sucked Bart harder and faster, Bart rubbed the ropes around his wrists harder against the concrete wall. He finally felt them loosening.

"Fucker," Bart whimpered. "Swear to you Mister, if I still had my pretty sheer socks on now I definitely would've jumped outa the stinkers, what with the way you're siphoning on my cock and all... UHHHHHH!"

The sounds of slurping at his cock was maddening for the overused football player at that point, and he was no longer feeling sexy in the least, he was feeling beyond violated and put upon.

Bart clenched his teeth as he felt what had to be the umpteenth dry load being cooked up in his poor balls.

"Fuck, man, y—you're gonna get my goddamned nut again," Bart sniveled, tears filling his eyes behind his blindfold.

"And your piss as well, dee-lite," the toothless man squabbled, and quickly used his tongue to suck Bart's steely erection back and deep into his greedy mouth. "Mmm..."

Bart screamed in a mixture of passion and pain.

About five minutes later, Bart felt himself being sucked of another dry load, and then the toothless man planning to make him piss yet again as the ropes fell away from his wrists, at long last.

"Fuck, fuck, fuck man, this is inhumane!!!" Bart thundered when the ropes fell from his wrists.

Bart quickly reached up, whipped the blindfold from his eyes and looked down at the man with his cock still in his mouth.

"Fucker!" Bart railed and literally, with the front of one of his huge hands, swatted the guy off his man-meat.

The toothless man made a sound of surprise as Bart's spent cock was practically torn from his craw.

The man's head hit the ground and he blacked out, remnants of saliva and a trickle of Bart's piss lilting on his mangy lips. As Bart caught his breath and his cock shriveled between his legs, he cursed, swore and spit on the homeless man numerous times.

"Bastard, how could you do that to me???" Bart thundered breathlessly.

A short while later, Bart exited the alley wearing nothing but a pair of pants he had found in one of the trash bins. He was elated to see that he was at the Cherry Hill Mall and quickly made his way back toward Calderfield College. One of the first things he would have to do is a have a real sit-down with his buddy, jock pussy, after he had showered for a few hours.

It was a couple of hours later when the Leviathan docked.

One by one, the galley slaves were released from their bonds by Zeb and the drummer and then lined up for inspection by Coach Wilkinson and the whip master.

Jock pussy simply stood there, his muscles sore and his back welted, wondering what would happen next. Jock pussy hadn't realized just how many times he had been whipped. He choked on his tears, wondering why Spike had signed him up for this.

Coach Wilkinson nodded to the drummer and the whip master. They grabbed jock pussy and forced him face down on a picnic table. Jock pussy did not resist as they quickly tied his arms to the tops and sides of the table, and his legs (spread wide) to the table's legs. At another nod from Coach Wilkinson, Zeb greased the handle of an oar. He then handed the oar to the whip master.

While the drummer steadied jock pussy's lower back, the whip master pushed the pommel into jock pussy's gaping hole. Jock pussy's head sprang up at the intrusion, but surprise and resistance soon gave way to pleasure, and jock pussy found himself gasping and groaning. The pommel was then pulled out, leaving jock pussy feeling a bit frustrated. The drummer yanked jock pussy's head up by a handful of his wavy, sweat-soaked hair. As jock pussy's mouth automatically dropped open, the whip master forced his cock inside, groaning as jock pussy began a rhythmic sucking motion the way Spike had taught him.

Jock pussy sucked away, only to have his handsome head pulled back again after a few minutes. The whip master walked around and shoved his now well-moistened cock into jock pussy's hole as the drummer pulled the jock's head up and stuck his cock in.

Jock pussy swooned as he was speared from both sides.

And for the next couple of hours, that was how jock pussy spent his time, working from stroke to bow, alternating left and right oars. He was made to service everyone, except Zeb and Coach Wilkinson.

After the galley slaves had had a few romps each with jock pussy's asshole and mouth, the drummer and the whip master marched them off, leaving jock pussy wondering where. Jock pussy also wondered who the hell was going to take care of his raging hard-on. He glanced up at Zeb and Coach Wilkinson, and jock pussy was not the least bit surprised, even though it did add to his frustration, as he watched Zeb kneel in front of the coach and suck him off.

After Zeb was done, Coach Wilkinson seemed more affectionate than domineering toward Zeb.

A short while later, jock pussy was released from the table. He began to jack himself off, but Zeb asked him if he had permission, grabbing the football player by a handful of his hair and herding him back to the car while jock pussy whimpered, "No."

"Then don't!" Zeb stated sternly. "The way I'm seeing this, Spike wants you to have the bluest case of blue balls in college boy history, just as Coach Wilkinson wants me to have."

"Look, man, its twice as bad for me," jock pussy said, looking imploringly at the man currently in charge of him.

"It should be easier for you, you mean, seeing as you're twice the man I am," Zeb said, glancing down at his one testicle.

Jock pussy doubted the logic of what the man had just said, but seeing that as an opening, he politely asked Zeb, "What, uh, what happened to your other ball?"

"Heh, I knew I left something back at the office," Zeb replied musingly.

Jock pussy looked at the man, a feeling of exasperation showing on his handsome face.

"Oh okay, I gave my other testicle to Coach Wilkinson," Zeb said.

"Huh?" jock pussy replied, looking at Zeb in disbelief. "Just because I'm a little befuddled about my lust for a skinhead's boots, do you think I'm some sort of an idiot?"

"No comment, sweet thing," Zeb replied.

"Look man, I would sooner cut my throat before I would cut off one of my balls for anyone, and that includes Spike," jock pussy railed.

"Well, if that's how you feel about it," Zeb began, but jock pussy stopped walking, pulled away from Zeb's grip on his hair and faced the man.

"How you feel about it???" jock pussy asked, glancing down again at Zeb's lone testicle.

"Truthfully, I feel good that I'm Coach Wilkinson's property, it does make me happy," Zeb said, looking adoringly at jock pussy and feeling just a few twinges of jealousy where Spike was concerned over this sweet thing. "You see, sweet thing, Coach Wilkinson uses me as he wants. And he also decides if, how, and when and with whom I cum."

"Spike doesn't control when I cum," jock pussy said, and the two young men resumed walking.

"Well, I don't know what the deal is between you and Spike," Zeb said. "I'm just assuming that in time, he will let you know *exactly* how he wants things; and I'm sure he'll let me know as well, seeing as he's appointed me as your trainer."

"Look, Spike doesn't control me," jock pussy began, but Zeb stepped in front of him and grabbed both his nipples in his big fingers and thumbs, twisting them meanly.

"Ow, hey man, easy with the tits, huh," jock pussy barked.

"Spike doesn't control you, huh, sweet thing?" Zeb asked meanly, twisting the tar out of jock pussy's nipples. "If Spike doesn't control you, then what the fuck are you doing here with me, naked and with a back welted with what can only be called badges of honor?"

"O—okay, okay, you got a point there," jock pussy squawked and

Zeb let go of his nipples.

When they'd reached the car, Zeb offered jock pussy the choice between trousers or trunk, explaining that if jock pussy chose the trousers then he could sit in the car with him, if he preferred to remain naked, then it was into the trunk he would go.

"That's an easy decision," jock pussy said and pulled a pair of trousers that had seemed to appear magically in the back seat of Zeb's car. "Hmmm, these are most definitely mine. But if I wear these and ride up front with you ,then I'll know where The Estate is."

Zeb smiled, watching as jock pussy pulled the gray trousers on.

"Well, you know about your football coach, I know you saw him earlier," Zeb said as jock pussy buttoned up his trousers. "Blackmail works both ways, huh, sweet thing?"

During the ride back, Zeb marveled at how erotically hot jock pussy looked wearing nothing more than just a pair of dress pants. While jock pussy leaned back comfortably in the passenger seat, the feeling of the soft seat pressed against his welted and whipped back, Zeb told the football player more about the history of The Estate.

"Here at The Estate, slaves are registered as property with inventory numbers," Zeb said to jock pussy as he drove, "such as the number that's tattooed on my chest along with Coach Wilkinson's brand."

As he spoke, though, Zeb glanced over and saw that jock pussy had fallen asleep in the passenger seat. He stopped the car for a moment, leaned over and gently kissed jock pussy's cheek, whispering, "Sweet thing, sweet beautiful thing…I hope Spike knows how lucky he is to have you," and then drove the rest of the way back to the team office.

Once back at the team office, Zeb and jock pussy found Spike waiting for them. At the sight of Spike, jock pussy's eyes opened wide with joy as he exclaimed, "Sir."

But Spike held up a hand, instantly silencing jock pussy. In front of Zeb, jock pussy snapped to a stance of attention.

Then, ignoring jock pussy, Spike asked Zeb, "So, how'd my boy here do with the training?"

At the sound of Spike calling him his boy, jock pussy's cock engorged to its full nine inches and tented the front of his gray trousers.

"To be honest, bud, it went very well," Zeb said to Spike. "There were no problems at all; he sure as fuck can take it. Jock pussy here could easily have a place on our varsity crew as well as his football team at Calderfield College."

"Heh, knowing this boy of mine, I don't believe there weren't any problems," Spike said meanly, sneering at jock pussy. "Okay jock pussy, permission to speak is granted."

"Thank you, Sir. I appreciate that, Sir," jock pussy intoned. "As trainer, Zeb said there were no problems at all, except for not being allowed to cum, that is. Seeing as I did find myself very aroused over a lot of the experiences, I really wanted to cum."

"Well, jock pussy, as of now, *there is* a new rule for you," Spike said, curling one of his big hands into a meaty and grimy fist. "From now on, you cum only when I say you can cum."

Jock pussy's eyes opened wide in shock as he glanced over at Zeb, who smiled meanly as Spike sunk a hard punch into jock pussy's balls.

Jock pussy roared in indescribable pain and, on impact, shot his load in his trousers.

He crumpled over in pain, gasping, heaving, and then, looking up at Spike, muttered, "Thank you, Sir."

A short while later, Spike was walking toward his pickup with jock pussy slung over one of his huge shoulders like a sack of laundry. Jock pussy's hands were tied tightly behind him, his upper arms were roped tight with the rope cinched around his upper body, making a nice showcase of his nipples. His legs were tied in three places and his bare feet were tied tight at the ankles. He was gagged with a pair of Zeb's white sweat socks, one sock crammed in his mouth, the other tied over it, jamming it securely in place. Jock pussy was wrapped and tied good and securely, like a gift, done expertly by Zeb himself as a present to Spike for allowing him to train the handsome sweet thing that day.

* * *

A few hours later, Travis walked into his dorm room, exhausted, his welted back smarting, his bare feet aching and in one hand the keys to his dorm room, which Spike had kept safe for him. In his other hand were Zeb's sweat socks, his souvenir of his time at Leo's Estate. As Travis closed the door to his dorm room, he called out, "Chad, are you here, buddy?" But when Travis turned from the closed door, he saw Bart Findley dressed casually in a pair of blue cargo shorts by The Gap, a white pull-over tee shirt by Nike and ankle length blue sweat socks with Nike sneakers.

"Bart, hey man, where have you been?" Travis asked, too exhausted and too out of it to note the way that Bart was taking in the sight of his disheveled state. "Is everything okay bud? Did Chad let you in while I was gone?"

"Well, Travis, bud, let's just say that you and I need to have a little talk, okay?" Bart said.

*An **ampallang** is a male genital piercing passing horizontally through the the entire glans of the penis.

CPSIA information can be obtained at www.ICGtesting.com
Printed in the USA
BVOW03s1001230114

342806BV00021B/676/P